Christmas
Notes

Tara

May these Christmas notes
enter your heart.

Chris G Cox

Bedside Books
An imprint of American Book Publishing
5442 So. 900 East, #146
Salt Lake City, UT 84117-7204
www.american-book.com
Printed in the United States of America on acid-free paper.

Christmas Notes

Designed by Jana Rade, design@american-book.com

Publisher's Note: This is a work of fiction. Names, characters, places, and inci-
dents either are the product of the author's imagination, or are used fictitiously, and any
resemblance to actual persons, living or dead, events, or locales is entirely coincidental.

ISBN-13: 978-1-58982-841-4
ISBN-10: 1-58982-841-0

Cox, Clint G., Christmas Notes

Special Sales

These books are available at special discounts for bulk purchases. Special editions, including
personalized covers, excerpts of existing books, and corporate imprints, can be created in
large quantities for special needs. For more information e-mail info@american-book.com.

Christmas
Notes

By Clint G. Cox

Dedication

I would like to dedicate this story to my children. While they do not fully understand why I work so hard, they never let me forget which priorities should be most important in my life: family, faith, and fun. May they never lose their hope in life.

Foreword

As a musician, I have had the opportunity to travel the world entertaining. I have shared my talents with many people through music and song. One of my hopes as I perform for people is that after the last note has been played, and the last word has been sung, I have left everyone in attendance feeling uplifted and in higher spirits than when they arrived for the show. I am always happy to introduce new talent who want to do the same.

I first met Clint G. Cox, author of *Christmas Notes*, when he came to my house to do some plumbing work. That's right; he is a plumber. Since then, I have recognized him as a neighbor, faithful religious brother, wonderful father, and now a talented writer.

His book, *Christmas Notes*, is an emotional, life-pondering story that teaches a grand Christmas message. *Christmas Notes* leaves readers with the same feelings that I want to leave with my listeners. Clint has used his talent to write a book that will not only help you feel the Christmas spirit, but will also remind you of those things most important in life. These reminders help make it possible to have the spirit of this magical holiday stay with you all year long. Clint does this through the main character, Seanna, an orphan girl with a very unique method of communicating. This little five-year-old girl gives recognition to everything that Christmas should be. It is amazing how a simple note can teach a life-altering message. If you struggle with feeling the magic of Christmas, or know someone who does, then this book is for you.

As an entertainer who loves to use music to uplift and strengthen people's lives, I gladly recommend Clint G. Cox as an author who wants to do the same for all those who read his writings, especially this book, *Christmas Notes*.

Merrill Osmond: Entertainer, Husband, and Father

P.S. If Seanna were to write me a note, it would say, *"Family,"* to remind me always of those at home who are my most adoring fans.

X _____

Preface

We all go through patterns during our lives that put us either closer to or further from happiness. Over the years, I have discovered that true happiness comes from our relationship with our family and from our faith. For this reason, I wrote this story for my children. I wrote it to help them realize that when it seems as if there is no hope, all they have to do is open their hearts and seek out what is most important. If we can all do this, then we will find a greater joy than we could ever imagine.

Even though this story is fictional, we can all relate to the feelings and patterns that the characters go through. It does not matter which point of the cycle we are in during our lives. If we can change our focus to the truths in life, then we can, and will, find joy. Although we may not always have a Seanna there to remind us of what is important, I do believe that if we keep our hearts open and look for the signs that will show us happiness, then we will certainly find the happiness we seek.

Christmas is the time of year when most people's hearts seem to be more open and more reachable. I hope this story will fill your heart with joy during this Christmas season and for years to come.

Thanks for reading.

Clint G. Cox

Introduction

Why is it that the world seems to change during the Christmas holiday season? People seem to be friendlier, family seems to be more on the mind, and, somehow, the worries of life seem to not weigh so heavy on the heart. Oh, I realize that perhaps it is not like this for everybody. It has not always been like that for me. In fact, it was just the opposite. I did not seem to care about this season at all. I just never gave much attention to it. I went through the motions that everybody expects you to: bought a tree, put lights on the house, and gave gifts to others. Then, one Christmas I received a special gift. It was not a tie, or sweater, or even a gadget that lights up and plays a tune. It was a person. A person who, in a very simple way, helped me understand the true meaning of Christmas, which in turn helped me learn the true meaning of life.

Chapter 1

As I drove slowly on the highway, towards the city, I could not help but feel as if this were just a big waste of time and money. I certainly was in no hurry to get to the orphanage. Jenny and I had always wanted to have a child in the house, though more for her than me; still, seeing her get so excited about the idea somehow made me excited, too. That was until June, when I lost my job. I have been out of work ever since. I have to admit that my self-esteem, attitude, pride and whatever else you want to add to that have been destroyed during the past six months. I had just been getting on top again, after making a huge mistake in my dad's business only two years earlier. I was responsible for my dad losing his biggest client. After basically destroying his business, I just handed him my resignation and left. We have not spoken since. I think Jenny has probably had some contact with my mother because she keeps trying to tell me I need to talk with my dad about what happened. I just cannot make myself do it. I humiliated him as a business owner, a friend, and a father. I do not know if I want to go through the pain of being a disappointment to him all over again.

After leaving Dad's company, I quickly found a new job. Men of my position were in high demand two years ago. I wish I could say the same right now. With the economy in such shambles and with so many other people out of work, I guess I am not as important as I thought. I have had interview after interview and searched job listing after job listing, but so far nothing has panned out. "Overqualified," was a frequent response I would get. All I wanted to do was work. How can you be overqualified for that? I would do anything. I have interviewed for everything, even the high school janitor position. I have found a few odd jobs to help pay some of the bills, and these helped keep me from going insane by just staring at the walls.

Jenny has been so supportive and, luckily, my dad did teach me something about finances. I have always been a saver, and we had a little nest egg built up. That savings is certainly getting smaller, even with Jenny taking those extra shifts at the nursing station in the children's cancer ward. She loves working with the children and is good at what she does. All those extra shifts have been taking a toll on her lately though. She seems to not feel good and looks tired all the time. She says she is fine, but she still worries me.

This Christmas season seemed to be following the same pattern of the last few we have spent together. Lately, they all just seemed like train wrecks. The holidays last year were terrible, to say the least. After years of trying, we finally learned that we could not have children of our own. In my feeble attempt to make Jenny feel better, I signed us up for a service program to take in one of the children from the local orphanage for the month of December. I thought it would be the perfect Christmas gift for her. We would get to buy a child Christmas presents, play Santa, and have a month of fun playing pretend family. I was so proud of myself for thinking of it. We decided that a younger child, about four or five, would fit us best. At that age, he/she would be past the terrible twos and potty-trained!

I still remember taking Jenny to the orphanage to get the process moving. I had no idea what I was in for that day. I expected that we would just fill out some papers, pick the child we wanted, and be on our way. I naively described it that way to Jenny, too. She was so excited! It was the first time I had seen her truly happy since the discussion with the fertility doctor. She was hoping for a girl. I was undecided. I was just excited to see her happy again. She even bought a magazine that showed how to fix different hairstyles for little girls. She was giddy discussing her favorite styles as we made the drive into the city.

When we arrived at the orphanage, I noticed several other couples there, probably for the same reason we were. The woman helping us, a Mrs. Hagar according to the badge, was in no mood for small talk, just business, as she directed us where to sign. She sat in her chair like a sergeant ready to bark commands at the next person who did something out of order. I guessed that she must have been from the state department, some sort of social worker cop. The uniform she wore gave that away. There was no way she could work at the orphanage. She kept giving the children in the room these death glances while they were waiting with their prospective holiday families.

"When do we go to pick out the child?" I asked, trying to break the silence after we signed the papers. The woman just smiled. The smile looked out of place on such a hard face. Whatever I said must have struck her funny bone because she was really straining her facial muscles trying not to laugh. She failed, and her laugh was even more awkward for her character. I looked over at Jenny to see if I was the only one who did not get the joke that I had apparently just made. Jenny just looked back at me with a concerned expression, as though this person in front of us could actually die from her strenuous outburst.

"Did you think you would get to take the child home to-day?" the woman asked, laughing harder. She started holding her side as if it were hurting her.

"Yes," Jenny said, now frowning. We could not believe that there was a year waiting list for these children. The woman explained that they use that time to try to find out as much about the couples as possible to make sure the children were not going to be in any danger. I should have found out more about the details of the process before telling my wife about the surprise. Jenny was a trooper though and managed to hold herself together until we got back into the car. It was yet another disappointment for us that Christmas.

Why has Christmas changed so much for me? I used to love it; now, it is nothing more than a time of dread and disillusionment. When I was a kid, my mom used to make Christmas so much fun, and I used to love the season. I remember making my list for Santa just after Halloween. Then, after Thanksgiving, we would start decorating. It was a magical time. Mom would set up the old nativity. She has had it for most of my life. I used to sit and stare at the pieces, always wondering why it was so important to have them out for Christmas. Occasionally, when Mom was not looking, I would play with them. Somehow, she always knew and chastised me afterwards. Surely, she has set it out by now this year.

A few weeks ago, we received news from the orphanage that we had passed their test, and there was a child available to stay with us this Christmas season. I had almost written off the idea of being able to do the holiday adoption. I figured that losing my job would have disqualified us. Jenny must have figured the same because, when she heard the news, she was elated. She just could not stop smiling and had already started calling girlfriends for supplies. I, however, could not get excited. The timing of it all just was not in my favor. Yet, here we are: me, out of work, driving into the city to bring a child home for Christmas.

I pulled up to the orphanage and parked in the parking space in front of the door. I had the same feelings looking at the building as I had the previous year when we first came to sign the papers. For a place that housed children, it did not look very inviting. The building had four stories and a façade that was reminiscent of Roman architecture. Judging by the old stone steps leading up to the front doors, this building was probably posh back when it was built. It was made of stone that was once bright yellow but now was a dull green from the elements. The stones under the archways still have the yellow finish. The windows looked like they were the originals from when the building was new. They almost gave it a spooky look. The orphanage had updated the doors with, commercial privacy glass. The building was smashed in between two backsides of modern-day office buildings; I recognized one as a big bank, and the other was the corporate building for some multimillion-dollar company. Both structures really made the smaller four-story building stand out.

I must have taken a slower drive than I thought; the sun had almost set, and it was getting late. There were only a few cars left in the parking lot, some of which were parked under the "staff only" signs. I parked under a dimly lit light. The staff cars had a thick dusting of snow on their hoods from the snowfall earlier in the day. The snow lent a quiet, serene feeling to the scene in front of me.

Even with the job loss, somehow I thought this would feel different and be more exiting. I was not excited at all. *How did I get into this mess?* It would definitely not turn out as I had planned. The plan was that Jenny was going to take the whole time off to be with the child, while I was going to work and then spend time with them when I got home in the evenings and on the weekends. Losing my job certainly messed that up; now it was the other way around. What was I going to do with a child for a whole month? What was I supposed to do if she had a lot of personal baggage? What would I do if she were a drug baby and not fully functional? Even if she were normal, then with my lack of parental experience, I was bound to return her broken. *I should just back up and leave.* Yeah right. Jenny would be so disappointed. That was all I needed to do to her. She would leave me for sure then. I was surprised she had not already. I had been such a failure......

Tap, tap, tap. I must have been sitting here awhile. A staff member was now standing at my car, her arms crossed either in frustration or maybe just to keep warm. I hoped it was the latter. I never even noticed her leaving the building. As I was getting out of the car, she asked, "Are you Mr. Fox?" She was a thin woman in her late thirties, dressed in what looked like a schoolteacher's uniform.

"Yes," I replied timidly. I felt as though I had been sent to the principal's office, and I had not even stepped foot inside the door yet. Still, she was better than the drill sergeant who had created such a scene the year before.

"I am Miss Hinder, the head staff member at this orphanage. You have a very anxious little girl waiting for you." She laughed irritably. I must have looked silly sitting out there talking to myself.

"Oh, I'm sorry I'm late."

"Only an hour," she said firmly. Wow, I have gotten good at killing time. Actually, I am a pro after doing it for five months, I thought to myself.

"Poor little thing. She's been on the verge of tears the whole time, afraid she had been forgotten," she scolded me.

"Oh, I'm sorry," I said, embarrassed.

"Don't apologize to me. It's her you need to apologize to," she lectured again.

"Great. I've already messed this up," I mumbled to myself. I stared nervously at the door.

"There's always one every year," she said, a little lighter.

"I'm sorry, one what?"

"One who needs this more than the children do," she said with a motherly grin on her face. I wanted to ask her what she meant by that, but I thought it best not to keep the child waiting any longer. I followed Miss Hinder across the mostly-emptied parking lot, up the faded stone steps, and into the large, quiet old building.

Chapter 2

Once we were inside the orphanage, I noticed that it was tidy and very clean but still appeared weathered by the occupants in its vast past and by the children whom it still housed. There was not a corner that was not chipped, a piece of furniture that was not ripped. The same stone on the outside was the finish wall on the inside. This stone, though, looked more yellowish, like those few pieces outside that were protected from the seasons. There were arched doorways with keystones at the top. If the room had had more light, then it probably would not have felt so cold. It looked like they had upgraded the heating though because the big stone fireplace appeared as if there had not been a fire in it for some time. It was a long building, which stretched out deep into the middle of the block. I could just make out what looked like a courtyard with a prison fence around it. The way the barbed wire was facing, though, it looked to be trying to keep people out, not in. It was hard to imagine that they were trying to raise all these children in such a rundown place.

"Please sit down, Mr. Fox," Miss Hinder said, pointing to a chair on the opposite side of the desk. It was the very same desk where Jenny and I had sat to sign papers the year before. As the memory hit me I glanced around, hoping not to see Mrs. Hagar, who would laugh me out of the building again. I sat down and immediately felt as though as I were about to check into a hotel. However, I was going to be checking a child out of this building. It was a very strange feeling.

"You are the last one, and I have had plenty of time to get your paperwork ready while waiting for you," she said with an irritation in her tone. I smirked sheepishly. She could have been an attractive woman if not for the look she always had on her face. It was a look like one my mom used to give me when I was in trouble or when she was just tired from a long day. I wondered if Miss Hinder was just giving me this look because of my tardiness, but judging by the lines on her face, this was a permanent expression. Perhaps it came from having to deal with all these children day in and day out.

"Your background check has already been completed, and your track record for the last year looks good. How is the job hunt going?" she said, looking into my eyes.

"Good, no leads as of yet though," I said, worriedly hoping this comment would not disqualify us from getting the child. I then began to wonder what else they knew about us from this past year. Mrs. Hagar was not kidding when she said they looked into your background during your year-long waiting period.

"Where is your wife? Usually the couple, or family, comes together to pick up the child," she said, extinguishing my thoughts of all the bad experiences that had happened over the past year.

"Jenny could not get her shift covered at the hospital," I said, feeling guilty for how I had messed this day up. My heart ached a little at saying these words as I thought of Jenny missing this part of the experience.

"I just need you to sign your name here and here." I took the pen and hesitated.

"Do I even get to see the child before I sign?" I asked.

"Will that make any difference?" she replied. I had to think about that for a second. It did not take long, as I thought of what Jenny's face would look like if I came home without a child.

"No, I guess not," I replied.

"Then sign here, please," she said, a little more compassionately. The way she said it, it sounded as if I had passed some kind of a test. I signed on the designated lines.

"Sharon, will you go and get Seanna? I am sure she is ready to go," she told a slim staff member with short blond hair who was standing behind me. I had not even noticed that Sharon was there. I wondered if she was standing there to stop me in case I tried to run.

"Yes, Miss Hinder," she said, walking away. Sharon looked about college-aged, which was logical because there was a local college a couple of blocks down the street. It was famous for turning out child psychologists. The orphanage would be an ideal place for a student to work while studying at the university. Sharon seemed good-natured and happy to be there.

While we were waiting, I took the liberty of finishing my onceover the best I could while sitting in my chair. I noticed there were no decorations or Christmas trees. There were just bare walls with some boring pictures on them. I guess that made sense. The children would all be gone for the holidays anyway. Judging by the water mixed with dirt on the floor, this had been a busy place today, with so many couples and families picking up the children. Some large rooms close to where we were sitting looked to be the kitchen and cafeteria. They looked as though they were once a fancy restaurant. The eating area was quite large; surely there were not enough children here to fill that entire room. *What do they do with the rest of the space?*

"Do you have any questions, Mr. Fox?" Miss Hinder asked, breaking my contemplation.

"Yes," I stuttered. How do I even start?

"Do you send someone to check on us?" I asked shyly.

"Do you need it?" She laughed.

"Look, I'm scared to death, if you haven't noticed. I'm not sure this is the best time for us, but my wife is excited," I admitted.

"Yes. Every week there will be a staff member who makes a house call. Sharon is your staff member. Look, I have been here at this orphanage for ten years, and out of all the children I have seen come here, Seanna is the one for whom I am least worried. She is something very special. I am going to miss her around here," she said in a rush.

"Why is she so special?" I asked.

"Oh, you'll find out," she said, smiling. Then I could hear footsteps coming.

"Is she ok?" I asked. "Sometimes when people say someone is 'special', they mean handicapped, you know," I said in a panic. She just smiled. There was no time for an answer. When Sharon and the little girl came around the corner, my heart was beating so hard that I was sure everybody could hear it.

Something happened as my eyes went from Sharon's face to Seanna. There is only one way to describe it: light. Picture a room that is calm and dim, almost dark, and in one corner there is a small bright light. A bright light is the best description I could give of Seanna. My mind tried to peg a memory of having seen a light around a child like this before, but I gave up after a second. Were my eyes playing tricks on me? Was there a noticeable difference that would have separated her from any other child? It was not because of what she was wearing. Her clothes, to put it nicely, were rags. She had on some old black dress shoes and cream-colored knee-high stockings. Her faded knee-length skirt looked like a kilt. Her coat was brown and looked like it was hand knitted, with a matching hat and gloves. They were probably from somebody's service project they had done for the orphanage. I noticed that the pockets of the coat were stuffed full of something. I could not help but think that Seanna was going to freeze once we went out into the cold. Yet, despite her appearance, she seemed to give an aura of peace. She passed by us almost at a happy trot, with her dark, curly, untamed hair bouncing under her hat as she went.

Seanna smiled at Miss Hinder, and I could not help but notice the deep dimples in her cheeks. She was beautiful. I smiled as she looked at me, but all I got from her was a dimpled smirk.

"I guess I deserved that," I coughed to Miss Hinder. Seanna went over to the big doors and stomped her feet. I looked at Miss Hinder, confused.

"Oh, I forgot to mention that she can't speak," she stated.

"What?" I asked.

"Oh, don't worry. She's very good at communicating what she wants and needs," she said confidently.

"You mean I have to spend a month with this little girl who can't talk?" I wondered why they had not told me this before. I was completely unprepared for a normal child, let alone one with this type of disability.

"Shh. She'll hear you," she replied.

"Was she born like that, or…" *Stomp, stomp, stomp.* Seanna stomped impatiently at the door.

"Sharon, could you play a game with her for a minute? Mr. Fox is having a panic attack," Miss Hinder said jokingly.

"Sss, sss, sss, sss," was the sound that came from Seanna's mouth. It sounded like what a snake would sound like if a snake could laugh. I looked at Miss Hinder with a puzzled expression.

"What? Everybody makes a sound when they laugh, and that's hers," she said. I could hear Seanna and Sharon start to play some sort of hand game.

"I'll tell you what we know. Okay?" she said, her voice turning grim.

"Okay," I said, staring at her, ready for the information I felt had been purposely withheld.

"About this time last year, during those bad snowstorms we had just after Thanksgiving, Seanna and her parents were in a car wreck. They must have just been passing through because nobody seems to know them here. I figure they were lost. Anyway, they were most likely college students headed home for the holidays. They were in a head-on collision, and Seanna's parents died instantly. They didn't have much with them, but it wouldn't have mattered. The fire destroyed everything. A brave 16-year-old boy pulled Seanna from the wreck just before the car burst into flames. He suffered severe burns on his face, back, and arms because he shielded Seanna from the flames. She wasn't burned at all. The car was completely destroyed; not even the license plate was readable." She wiped a tear from her eye before continuing.

"They figured, from what the teenager said, that Seanna must have been sleeping slumped in the car seat, with the seat belt in a bad spot against her throat. The impact crushed her throat so badly that, once the surgeries were over, she was left without vocal cords." I looked over at the two girls playing games, and I saw something on Seanna's neck that I had failed to notice before. I could barely see the top of a scar. It started under her chin and went behind a scarf she was wearing, probably to hide it. She looked at me and pulled the scarf up to her chin, shooting me a worried look. I deeply regretted my comment about the "month with a girl who can't talk," and I hoped that she had not heard me.

"Poor girl, she's worried people will not want her because of her scar. That and because she can't talk," Miss Hinder said with compassion. "She was thinking that you had found out and weren't coming when you were so late." She looked at me with an irritated expression.

"She doesn't have any other family?" I asked, changing the subject.

"The county and state authorities have done everything possible, but they don't have much to work with," she frowned.

"How do you know her name?" I asked.

"She was wearing a necklace that had that name on it. We're still unsure if it is her real name because, in the past year, nobody has inquired about a four-, now five-, year-old with that name," she answered.

"Does she know what happened to her mother and father?" I asked urgently.

"Yes, but you have to remember that she is only five, and without being able to talk, she has given no clues. Poor thing, this has to be so frustrating for her," she paused, wiping another tear before continuing.

"So, when the authorities figured they had done all they could do, they brought her here. Seanna is very special and smart. If I did not know any better, I would say she could read. She spends a lot of time looking at books; she loves children's books. Some of her favorites are children's books about the Bible. Once in a while, she'll write some of the words from her favorite stories on a piece of notepaper. She takes the notes everywhere she goes and gives them to people when she sees that they have a need for them. You have to be very special to get a note from her." I looked back at Seanna. That explained the bulges in her pockets. Seanna stood up, looking bored with the game, and stomped her feet.

"Does she come with an instruction manual?" I asked hopefully.

"No, she does not, Mr. Fox. It's time for you to go now. She's been patient long enough," Miss Hinder said tenderly.

"Okay. I know I'm in trouble, but I'm sure my wife will know what to do. So the faster we get to her, the better," I choked.

"Mr. Fox, don't think of it that way. Enjoy this experience so that Seanna can, too. I've seen miracles come out of this program of Orphans for the Holidays. You just have to open your heart and let them happen."

I stood up, walked over to Sharon and Seanna, and asked shyly, "Are you ready?" Seanna rolled her eyes, and for the first time I realized they were the same deep, beautiful brown as Jenny's eyes.

"That means 'Yes,' Mr. Fox, and I think you're on her naughty list, which means no notes for you," Sharon said, laughing. Seanna hissed her hissy laugh. It was cute the way her body wiggled when she laughed. It reminded me of a little Santa Claus laugh. I could tell the body language of hers was going to come in handy for communicating with her.

"Well, then, let's go," I said with my voice shaking.

"Are you ready?" Sharon asked me.

"Yes. I'll do my best."

"It's not a football game, Mr. Fox," she said, smiling. Seanna laughed.

"Let's go. I've kept you waiting long enough," I said, smiling back.

We started walking toward the doors, and Seanna hesitated. Has she changed her mind? I wondered. Maybe she doesn't want to come with me. I suddenly felt very disappointed and sad. It had never occurred to me that she might change her mind. Seanna must have seen the distress on my face, so she smiled. I melted. I hoped to see that smile a lot over the next month. Seanna spun around and ran back to the staff members. She hugged them both at the same time. Then, she pulled out a note written on yellow paper from inside a plastic bag in her coat pocket and gave it to Miss Hinder. Sharon read it aloud, "Thanks." The light that seemed to emulate around Seanna got brighter. Was I the only one who could see it?

"That's what's in my heart too, for having known you, Seanna, and I will remember to give thanks this Christmas. That is a beautiful Christmas note. Thank you," Sharon said tears filling in her eyes.

"Mine, too," Miss Hinder added, sobbing. I could tell there was a definite relationship of gratitude between these three, one that I had only seen before between close family members. Suddenly, I thought of Jenny. I have been such an ungrateful person lately, especially to her. She has really been a trooper these last couple of months, and I don't think I have thanked her once. How could I have been such a terrible husband?

I cleared my throat. The staff members looked irritated with me. They acted as though they were never going to see Seanna again. It's only a month, I thought. Seanna wiped tears from her eyes, too. She turned and walked back to me with that excited trot I had seen earlier. Suddenly, I was very excited and I had no idea why. My situation had not changed while I had been there. Yet, somehow I was excited nonetheless. I could not help but wonder if I would get a note. If I did, what would it say? As we walked to the car, all I could think about was that I wanted to do anything I could just to please this little girl.

Chapter 3

Reality finally set in again after we had been in the car for a minute or so. I had not said one word to Seanna, and the silence was starting to get uncomfortable. How was I going to do this? I have a hard time carrying on a conversation with an adult, let alone a mute five-year-old. Well, I had better try, or this could be a long month for the both of us. I looked in the rearview mirror. Seanna was sitting in the car seat that we had borrowed from one of Jenny's friends at work.

Oh, that reminded me; I needed to call Jenny to let her know I had picked up the child. We had had no idea what the gender of the child would be, so Jenny had several people at work who had older children tell her they would let her borrow anything she needed. Cindy, the woman who let us borrow the car seat, had some older daughters and was looking to get rid of some of the toys and clothes her girls had outgrown. I was sure Cindy was going to be happy we ended up with a girl.

"Hi, you hunk," Jenny answered her phone. I laughed. I loved it when she answered the phone this way; it always meant she was in a good mood and not mad at me.

"How are you?" I said, as though I really needed to ask.

"Do you have her?" she replied.

"How did you know it was going to be a girl?"

"It's a girl. Wahoo!" she screamed. I had to take the phone from my ear before my eardrum blew.

"Sss, sss, sss, sss," drifted a laugh from the back seat. I looked in the rearview mirror and saw those penetrating brown eyes and the dimples, accompanied with a smile, looking at me.

"Yes!" I could hear someone say in the background as Jenny announced the news. Great, I thought to myself as I registered who it was.

"Tell Cindy it's only for a month, and we only need some basics to get us by," I said loudly, hoping she would hear me. There came a whimper from the back seat. I looked in the rearview mirror again, but the bright eyes and dimples were gone. Seanna was slumped back into the car seat, staring out of the window into the dark, snowy night.

"Does she need anything?" Jenny said excitedly.

"Um, she has a small suitcase about one foot by one foot, but I didn't look to see what's inside."

"Ok, that means she needs everything then." I could tell by her voice that Jenny was smiling.

"No, it doesn't," I started to say but was cut off.

"We're just leaving the hospital. I'll follow Cindy to her house and get some stuff."

"Wait."

"I'll be home in one hour. Love you. Bye."

"Jenny," I said into thin air. I did not get a chance to tell her what I really wanted to. "She can't talk," I mouthed, looking out my window.

I looked into the rearview mirror again. Seanna was still looking out of the window. Was that a tear on her cheek? *Did I do something wrong? Is it because she's so happy to be out of the orphanage? Or maybe is it all the pretty lights on the houses?* We were out of the city now, driving past the huge, fancy homes in the suburbs. Many of the homes were in gated communities and were massive. And, by the looks of their lights, they were all trying to win the "best decorated holiday home" contest. It looked magical with the falling snow. The trees looked like they were growing marshmallows on their branches! The rolling hills in the distance were a silvery white from the first snowstorm. After being in that rundown, old orphanage, this must be quite a sight. With how decorated these houses were and the number of lights they had put up, these people must have really been in the Christmas spirit. Our lights were still down in the unfinished basement. Last year I did not feel like putting lights up, and I was too busy the year before. I was sure the lights were a tangled mess by now. *Is it even worth doing it this year either?*

I have had a hard time with the whole "Christmas" season. My parents were religious people and had dragged me to church occasionally. Every year when I was young, my mom tried to teach me about the true meaning of Christmas. It seemed so easy to believe back then. I did not know what to believe anymore. It was not as if I were a humbug or anything. I still went through the motions: attending one Christmas party here, another one there, saying a "Merry Christmas" here and there, shopping for gifts, spending a little money here, a lot of money there. Numb. I am just numb. I have no excitement and no thrill for this time of year. I try to put on a good face, though, for those around me, especially Jenny. She loves Christmas. Even last year she managed to find some spirit.

I realized we were almost home when I saw the church near our house in the distance. I had not said one word to Seanna during the 20-minute drive. I looked in the mirror again. She was perched up in her seat with her face glued to the window, so close that her breath was fogging it up, and she had to keep wiping it off. We were just coming over the bridge and a little river flowed underneath. The banks were still lined with thick snow-covered vegetation, although most of the trees and other plants in the area had died from the recent frosts. The river separated our smaller, less opulent suburban homes from the richer, grander houses.

As we crossed the bridge, Seanna started clapping and bouncing in her seat. I assumed from her body language that she was excited. On the front lawn of the church was a life-size scene of the nativity that was lit with a spotlight. The way the pieces in this nativity were faded it looked like the church had placed them out there every year, but I had never noticed them before; I drove by this spot almost every day. Numb, I tell you.

"Um, have you thought of what you want to ask Santa for Christmas?" This was my feeble attempt to talk to Seanna during the last two minutes of the trip. She bobbed her head, "Yes."

"What?" I don't know what I expected her to do; she couldn't tell me anyway. She looked at me in the mirror with a look that I could only describe as anticipation.

"Let's see if I can guess. A dolly?" She huffed, and the look now turned to frustration.

"Okay, no doll. A princess dress?" Seanna sat back in her seat, giving me a "You're hopeless" look. I tried a couple more guesses and finally gave up when it looked like she was going to cry. Thankfully, we were only a block away. *Yeah, she hates me. This is going to be a long December.* I sighed.

We pulled into the driveway as the garage door was still opening. Our home was not the smallest in the neighborhood, but it was not the largest either; it seemed enormous, though, with just the two of us living there. All of the homes in this part of the subdivision were of the same design, except for the exterior finish and interior décor. The homeowners designed those areas during construction. Jenny wanted pink stucco, but I had to put my foot down on that. After she had stamped out my black cobblestone idea, we were able to settle on a tan color with some flat stone on the bottom. The interior was all Jenny. I did not even want to fight about that. Overall, we had done our best to make it a good home, and we loved it, but there was just something missing. It never felt like the happy home that I remembered from my childhood.

Once inside the house, I realized that Jenny would not be home for another 45 minutes. What was I going to do to entertain this little girl for 45 minutes? Seanna stood in the entryway, looking around.

"A tour," I said. That will take some time. I started in the living room, describing it and then moving on to each room; I moved at a slower pace than on a normal tour that I would give somebody else. Seanna quickly became bored. She did think our master tub was cool, probably because it was so big, the room she liked the most was the one I described to her as *her* room. I had no idea why. There wasn't much of anything in there but blank walls and a twin bed with no sheets on it. She did not seem to mind though. She went in and sat down on the bed, giving me a "That's comfortable" look. Then I heard her belly rumble. I bet she hasn't eaten dinner yet. I looked at the clock: 6:15 pm. I bet she's starving.

"Next stop is the kitchen," I said, smiling. Seanna jumped off the bed and trotted over to me.

"Are you hungry?" I asked. Seanna looked at me with a deep, dimpled smile.

"I think I know just the thing to cure those belly rumbles," I said happily. It was nice to see her smile again. When we got to the kitchen, I showed her the pantry. I told her that there were plenty of treats if she got hungry.

"I'll fix some Mac and Cheese for you now, if you'd like." She stuck her tongue out and licked her lips. Just as I thought, every kid likes Mac & Cheese. Good thing too, as that is about all I can cook.

As we were about to finish dinner, I heard Jenny pull into the driveway. I looked at Seanna to see if she had noticed. She was still hunched over her plate, with one arm in the position of guarding the plate and the other one shoveling her third helping into her mouth. I wondered if she liked it that much, or if she was just really hungry. I could tell she was oblivious to the fact that Jenny was home.

"Is it all right if I go and check on something for a minute?" I asked. She nodded but did not miss a beat.

As I came outside, I saw Jenny lift up the back hatch of the SUV. The cargo lights came on, and my worst fears were confirmed. There was not one inch of room to spare.

"Hi, Honey, did you get enough stuff? Because I think you missed some space right there against the ceiling," I said, pointing at the top of the pile.

"Shoot, I did? Where?" she joked. She leaned in to give me a kiss. She's beautiful, I thought to myself. I could not help but notice, that her stunning brown eyes looked tired. Excited, but tired.

"There's plenty more where this came from," she said as though she had just hit a discount rack of name brand clothes.

"She's only going to be here for a month," I reminded her.

"I know, but I don't want to have our home look like the orphanage. Do you?"

"Good point," I said, giving in to her. That was usually how our arguments went. Jenny has a way of thinking things through better than I do. She looked happy, but dead on her feet.

"Are you feeling okay?" I asked, concerned.

"I'm fine. Just a little sick," she said, not wanting to ruin the moment.

"I think I make you sick," I joked, not wanting to spoil her excitement either.

"I think you're right," she said seriously. "Love sick," she added, smiling, giving me a kiss. I loved it when she was excited.

"Jen, we need to talk about Seanna," I said seriously.

"Her name is Seanna? What a beautiful name." I had not thought about it, but it was a very pretty name. "Is she cute? What color is her hair? Is it long or short?" she asked as she continued to load my arms with toys and clothes.

"She can't speak," I blurted out. I did not want to ruin Jenny's good mood, but I knew she would be upset if I let her greet the child unaware.

"She what?" she said, stunned.

"She was in an accident, and.....," I trailed off after noticing Seanna in the doorway. Jenny turned to look. The little girl looked sad and frightened by what I had just said. How could I mess this up any more?

"She's a doll!" Jenny said joyfully.

"Seanna, this is Jenny, my wife," I said apologetically.

"Seanna, you are the cutest little girl I've ever seen, and I love your name," Jenny said in a motherly voice. That is all it took. Seanna came sprinting off the stairs and ran straight into Jenny's outstretched arms. Something came over me as I witnessed Jenny hugging her. *Is this what a father feels like to see his wife hugging and comforting one of their children?* Whatever it was, I liked it and hoped it would stay for a while. Jenny stood up and carried Seanna into the house, telling her about all the stuff she had brought for her room. Seanna seemed to be glowing again. I stood there, stunned at how Jenny handled Seanna. It was so natural for her. *That's not fair. They're best friends, and they have known each other all of one minute. Jenny is a natural. I am such a mess -up.*

I was exhausted after I had carried all the items into Seanna's room. It took fifteen trips, and the room was not that big. The girls were in the kitchen getting Jenny something to eat. Jenny was as giddy as a schoolgirl, chatting with Seanna as if she were a playmate. I had not seen her act this way since the day before our wedding. I must have been some smooth talker to get such a beautiful, wonderful woman to marry me. I hoped she did not regret her decision.

"Tomorrow, maybe you can help "Mr. Scrooge" put up the Christmas tree and lights," Jenny said teasingly when she noticed me watching them from the living room. Seanna laughed her hissy laugh.

"That is so cute," she mouthed to me.

"Ba humbug," I teased back.

"Boo, boo," Jenny said, and Seanna motioned with her thumbs pointing down.

"Oh, all right. But no fair ganging up on me like that; I'm outnumbered," I said defiantly. Seanna laughed harder.

Jenny and Seanna spent the next two hours decorating Seanna's room, giggling and laughing the whole time. I cleaned the kitchen and then sat in the living room. I half-heartedly read the paper and mail, waiting for them to finish. When they were done, they *both* looked like they were ready for bed. Jenny yawned as they walked out of Seanna's room and into the bathroom. Seanna was in a faded nightgown. She looked cute. For the first time, I got a good look at that scar that went from her chin to her bosom. That had to be painful. Seanna covered her neck with her hands when she saw me looking and disappeared into the bathroom.

When Jenny and Seanna were finished in the bathroom, I could hear them getting to know each other in what sounded like a girls' powwow in Seanna's room. I wanted to go in, but I still had no idea of what my boundaries were, being a male. Jenny has it easy, I thought. I felt left out. I wanted to be with them the whole night, but I realized that girls needed time alone, and I was not sure if Seanna really trusted me anyway.

"Max, can you come here, please?" Jenny said from the bedroom, a hint of worry in her voice. I jumped out of my chair, very happy for the invite. When I got to the door, the girls were kneeling by the bed.

"Are you both okay?" I asked, looking perplexed.

"Yes. She wants us to pray together." I looked at Jenny with terror on my face.

"Pray?" I mouthed.

"Yes, pray. You do know how, don't you?"

"Um, sure. but it's been a while," I said, dropping to my knees beside Jenny next to the bed. Seanna pointed at me.

"You want me to say it?" I asked. She nodded.

"Are you sure?" I moaned. She nodded again. Jenny bumped me with her elbow.

"Okay, okay," I said. I took a deep breath and started my prayer.

"Our Father in Heaven, hallowed be Thy name. Thy Kingdom's fun. Let Thine power rain down on Earth as it is raining in Heaven. Forgive our debts as we pay them. Thy Kingdom come, I'll be done. Amen." There was nothing but giggles and hisses. I was clearly embarrassed. I was pretty sure that was the worst prayer ever offered. Seanna shook her head in disgust, and then she pointed to Jenny. I gave her a "Let's see if you can do better" look. She recited the prayer perfectly and then smiled at me.

"Show off," I coughed. Seanna frowned at Jenny too, which took her by surprise.

Seanna then bowed her head. Silence filled the room. I could not help but notice the glow around her. I was sure Jenny could see it, too. As I watched her, I could tell this was not a memorized prayer, but one that came from the heart of a child. She was so deep in thought and silence. Could God have really been listening? I wondered what her heart was saying. I had a feeling-Who knows why?-that she mentioned me in that prayer. After she was done, Seanna crawled into bed, and we tucked her in between the warm sheets. We stood up, and Jenny, with tears in her eyes, kissed Seanna on the head and said good night. I stood there stunned. All I could do was smile, or I would have cried, too. As we were leaving the room, Jenny stopped to turn out the lights and said, "Seanna, I love you." Seanna slid out of bed and ran over to her old coat. She searched through a couple of those notes in her pocket before grabbing one. She ran over to Jenny and gave it to her, smiling.

"Mother," Jenny read out loud. She burst into tears.

"Thank you," she said, hugging Seanna. I bet Jenny never thought that someone would call her that name, not after the devastating news we had received the year before. I too had thought that I would never hear Jenny be called a mother. For some reason, the reality of our not having children became very real to me in that moment. What would we miss out on by not being parents? My heart stuttered when I thought of my own mother and how much I admired and looked up to her. If there was one person in this world that deserved that kind of motherly admiration, it was Jenny.

Chapter 4

After Jenny tucked Seanna back in her bed and was in our room, she said, "She is such a doll."

"That is totally unfair that she gave you a note. I think she hates me," I complained.

"What are all the notes about that she is carrying in her coat pockets?" Jenny asked curiously. I was then finally able to tell her everything that had happened to me that afternoon.

"What a horrible thing to happen to a four-year-old," she said somberly.

"Yes, I know. And now she's stuck with me for a whole month. I totally destroyed today. What am I going to do with her for the next four weeks?" Jenny came over to me and sat next to me on the bed.

"Despite how you feel about yourself, you are a good man, and you will do just fine with this little angel," she said, looking at me with those deep brown eyes. I could see the joy and excitement in them, but at the same time, she looked exhausted. I gently kissed her.

"I really do love you," I said timidly. "I'm sorry how bummed I've been lately. I just didn't think it would take this long to find another job. Now I've ruined this experience. This should be your time to spend with her, not mine. It's no wonder you got a note from her. You're perfect with her," I said sorrowfully.

"Max, I love you. Seanna is going to fall in love with you, just as I did. Just be yourself and try to enjoy this little girl," Jenny sighed while falling asleep. After about fifteen minutes, I climbed out of bed to check on Seanna. She was sound asleep. There truly was something special about her. That talk with Jenny really helped. Now, I was excited again to spend some more time with Seanna.

I did not sleep much that night. I was trying to plan what the next day would be like. I thought I had it figured out around 2:00 am, and I finally fell asleep. It seems like I was not asleep long, though, when I heard Seanna's bedroom door open and her footsteps coming to our room. They stopped at our door. I lifted my head to see if it was a dream. She was standing there with eyes wide open and a big smile on her face. I looked at the clock-6:00 a.m. *Are you kidding me?* I was used to getting up early when I was working, but I had been slacking off lately. I was now accustomed to getting up when Jenny's alarm went off at 7:30 am. I climbed out of bed to see if everything was okay, being careful not to wake Jenny up. After putting on my robe, I met Seanna in the doorway.

"Is everything okay?" I asked. She just grinned and nodded. "Great," I thought. I could tell this was part of her routine. There was no way I was going to coax her back into bed.

"Are you hungry?" She nodded. We went into the kitchen and got her some cereal. She chose Apple Jacks. There was not much of a choice.

"Shopping!" I said aloud. That's another activity we need to do today. That's what we will do to fill the last couple of hours before Jenny gets home. Seanna ate her cereal with the same determination that she had the Mac & Cheese. I poured some for myself as well, and sat down to eat with her.

While we were eating, I decided to see how well she could understand me. I came up with a guessing game. She would either point at something or draw a picture of it with a pencil and paper. It was fun for both of us. When Jenny walked in on us, all dressed for work, we were laughing at a drawing Seanna was making of a horse that looked more like a monkey. I did not even realize that it was almost 8:00 am.

"Did you sleep well?" Jenny asked Seanna. Seanna wrapped her arms around herself as though she were cuddling.

"I told you my old bed was comfortable," Jenny said, smiling. "Have you decided what you're going to do today?" she asked, looking at me and raising her eyebrows.

"Yes. Mr. Grinch's heart grew three sizes last night, and he has decided to decorate," I said sarcastically. Seanna laughed excitedly.

"Good for the Grinch!" Jenny said, just as excited. "After I eat, we'll get you ready, Seanna." Jenny held her tummy as though she were not feeling well. I told her about the game we were playing and then went to get myself ready for the day. I could hear them playing as I went into the bedroom.

After Jenny had left to go to work, Seanna and I headed down to the basement to get the Christmas decorations. It took a while to find them all. I had no idea why we had so many. Apparently, I had not always been such a stick-in-the-mud towards Christmas. When I carried the last box out of the basement, Seanna looked relieved. I could tell she did not like the unfinished basement much.

"I remember being scared of my basement, too, when I was younger," I told her. "My dad said there was nothing to be scared of, but I just knew there was something down there that wanted to eat me!" Seanna ran ahead of me and beat me to the top of the stairs. I laughed.

"I was just kidding," I joked.

My thoughts turned to my dad. After my teenage years and graduation, I guess he figured he was through raising me, and our relationship changed. Maybe it was partly because I stopped thinking I was smarter than he was and could see I needed his wisdom. It was more like we were friends; we did everything together. I wondered if he was still mad at me over the company disaster. I felt an urge to share Seanna with him but was unsure if that were a good idea. I missed spending time with him. Even working with him had become a plea-sure. I also really missed the advice he always used to give me. I was sure he would give me some pointers about how to act around Seanna, which might earn me one of those notes. I pushed the thought aside as Seanna's warm hand touched mine. She must have noticed the change in my mood. Somehow, I think she knew I was sad.

We decorated for four hours before stopping for lunch. We got a lot done, but there was still quite a bit more to do. Seanna was such a good helper. I could tell she was enjoying every minute. Most of the inside decorating was done, including the tree. I let Seanna hang all of the decorations on the tree, which was why it looked so bottom-heavy.

"After we have lunch, we'll put up the outside lights," I told her as I started to cook the Mac & Cheese again. I was glad she had picked the same thing to eat as last night.

After we finished, I could tell Seanna was not going to make it outside with me to put up lights. Her beautiful brown eyes were having a hard time focusing on the last bites of her third helping. It was probably a good thing because when I looked at the thermometer, it showed 12 degrees Fahrenheit outside. I gently wiped Seanna's mouth, picked her up, and carried her to bed. She did not protest at all. I think she was asleep as soon as I picked her up. I hesitated at the side of her bed, the weight of her body felt good in my arms. I looked at her still face, and somehow in that moment my life felt like it had more meaning to it. I felt as if her safety and well-being was all that mattered, and my little dramas in my life had little importance. Is this what being a father feels like, love yet overwhelming concern? It was similar to the feelings I used to have when Jenny was in my arms: uneasy yet peaceful, something that had long since been absent from me. I stood in this atmosphere for a couple more minutes, not wanting it to end before putting her in bed. I then headed outside to put the lights up by myself.

I had just finished hanging the last of the lights and setting all of the timers when Seanna woke up and came to find me. I realized that I had taken longer than I thought and had probably let her sleep too long. I could tell she was a little disappointed that I had hung the outside lights without her, but I knew that I had done the right thing. I was frozen after spending so much time out in the cold.

"Did you have a good nap?" She stretched her arms up and nodded her head.

"Do you want to go to the grocery store?" She smiled a very excited smile and ran to get her coat and gloves. Even though Jenny had borrowed a hand-me-down coat from her friend at work, Seanna came out with the one she was wearing when I picked her up at the orphanage. I was about to ask her to go and put on the other one when I noticed the plastic baggies hanging out of the bulging pockets. I decided that even though it was rough-looking, it was probably warm enough.

"The lights will be on when we get home. We'll have to hurry, though, to beat Jenny home so we can surprise her." I said. Seanna clapped her hands enthusiastically.

We drove into the city to the grocery store on Center Street. The parking lot was clear full of cars because of "Shop with a Cop Day," the state-driven event to help children in need get Christmas gifts.

"If I had known this was today, I wouldn't have come," I mumbled. I looked in the rearview mirror, only to see that Seanna had heard me and had a disappointed look on her face.

"Well, we've come this far, so we might as well go shopping." We had to park a couple of blocks away from the store. While walking to the store, we went past an alley that was between two main street shops. Seanna froze and looked down the alley. I caught a glimpse of what she was looking at before pushing her forward. There were three homeless men huddled up to a metal barrel with a fire in it. Seanna shivered. I assumed she did so because of the dark alley. It made our basement look like a friendly fairyland.

We walked into the store. It was such a sight! There were grownups and children everywhere. Judging by the looks of how many children were there, I would say I was not the only one without a job. I felt bad for all those parents who were out of work and struggling to put food on the table, let alone buy Christmas gifts for their kids. *That's one advantage of not being able to have kids. Not having to worry about things like this*, I thought. That thought made my heart ache. Actually, I would rather be able to have kids and struggle every day if I had to than be dealt the hand that we had been given.

"Stay close to me," I said as we started our shopping.

The store was so crowded that I kept bumping into people. It looked like most of the parents seemed about as excited as I was to be there. Even with the crowds, I managed to get what I needed quickly. We were almost done when a police officer came up and asked if he could help Seanna get a toy as part of the "Shop with a Cop" charity event. I hesitated, and I was about to say that it was not necessary, but Seanna grabbed the cop's hand and led him to the toys. She picked out a small race car and then ran to the next aisle, dragging the cop with her, to get some snow gloves.

"Is that all?" the cop asked. Seanna nodded.

"Okay, this one was easy to please." He led her up to the cash register, and they checked out. I followed them. The last items that I needed were next to the toys. I was now finished too.

While the clerk was scanning my groceries, I thought about the gifts Seanna had picked out. The gloves I could understand. Her brown ones that matched her coat were starting to get holes in them. The race car, though, was not a typical girl present. I figured that Jenny must have spilled the beans about my hoping to get a boy from the orphanage, and this was Seanna's attempt to reconcile with me. After I paid the cashier, I looked over to where Seanna had been standing, but she was gone. At first I stayed calm, but after I had searched the store, running through the crowds of people, I started to panic. She's a five-year-old little girl who could not speak or scream, and that was what was worrying me the most. As I ran around the store looking for her, I had to keep pushing the horrible thoughts of someone kidnapping her out of my head. Fear was taking over. I couldn't believe I lost her. Panic hit me again. *Wait. Now just calm down and think, Max. If you were a little girl and got lost, where would you go? She might have gone to the car.* I grabbed my cart and hurried outside toward where we had parked.

As the car came into view, I still did not see Seanna, so I turned back toward the store again. *What have I done? Where could she be?* Then, out of the corner of my eye, I saw her at the end of the alley, standing next to the three scary men we had seen earlier. I ran for her at a full sprint, still pushing the shopping cart; it was making a loud, clattering sound from the one wobbly wheel. I called out, "Run, Seanna! I'm coming! Run to me! Run!"

I stopped ten feet short of the metal fire barrel, dead in my tracks. The three adult, rough-looking men all had tears running down their faces. They passed a little yellow note from one to the other. They all looked at me with an, "It's okay," look to let me know that there was nothing to be worried about. I looked at Seanna. The fire from the barrel lit up the end of the dark alley, but her countenance seemed to be brighter. She was standing by the barrel with her hands over it, trying to get warm. I slowly approached the group. The men hung their heads in shame, sobbing. This little girl sure had a knack of making grown-ups cry.

I gently asked the men, "What does it say?" I knew full well the power of those notes. Only one of the men was composed enough to talk.

"Hope," he whimpered.

"That's something we've all forgotten about," another man whispered, wiping a tear from his cheek.

"It's time we start hoping again," the last one mumbled. Then Seanna left the barrel and went over to a pile of boxes. She bent down, took the gloves and the racecar out of her pockets, and set them next to a little boy who was about her age and was sleeping in one of the boxes. I must have missed seeing the boy as we walked by the first time. Seanna, however, had not. That was probably what made her stop in the first place when I had pushed her on towards the store.

Seanna came back to me and grabbed my hand, giving me an "Okay, I'm ready to leave this spooky alley" face. She had used the same face when we were down in my basement, only this was ten times worse. It had taken a lot of courage to come here and do what she did.

"That's one special girl you have there," one of the men said.

"Yes, I know," I replied. Seanna smiled. Each man bent down to thank her for restoring their hope in life and in themselves. The last one to do so also thanked her for the gifts she had given his son.

"I need to get him out of this mess. I guess I've just given up on everything since his mom left us," he said. Seanna gave him a look of urgency.

"You're right. First thing tomorrow, we'll get on a bus back to my parents' place; I promise you that." He was barely able to speak; he was so emotional.

"I bought some extra food. Will you take some?" I said, motioning to my cart. I had bought a lot of food because I was not sure what Seanna liked.

"We would be much obliged," one man said. I gave them some food, and we said good-bye.

Walking out of the alley and back to the car, I remembered how good it felt to give to others in need, something I had not felt for a while. Lately, it seemed as if I were the needy one. *What has happened to me the last couple of years?* Perhaps I had lost my hope in life. *I have been so selfish. I have missed so much by chasing money and wallowing in my own self-pity.* I was suddenly extremely grateful for this little girl who was teaching me, one note at a time, what the Christmas season was all about again.

Once we got back into the car, I noticed the difference in temperature by the car compared to the alley. It was at least thirty degrees warmer in the alley because of all the heat that radiated from the buildings' vents that discharged into the alley. I made Seanna promise she would always make sure that I knew exactly where she was. She looked comforted that I cared so much and guilty for not telling me her plan. She agreed with a cross-my-heart motion, and I was satisfied.

Seanna clapped delightedly when she saw the lit Christmas lights on the house as we pulled into the driveway. I had to admit the lights did look good.

"Not bad for a Scrooge," I said grumpily.

"Sss, sss, sss," Seanna laughed. Jenny had beaten us home and was waiting at the door when we got out of the car. Seanna trotted excitedly into her arms.

"Do I get a hug too?" I asked sheepishly.

"Anybody that decorates this well for Christmas deserves a hug and a kiss," she laughed, giving me a big smacker on the lips.

"I'll have dinner waiting for you as soon as you empty the SUV," she said, killing the mood.

"What, more stuff?" I groaned.

"Relax. It's just some toys and books."

"Okay, but dinner better be good to soften me back up," I joked.

After we ate, we went through the same routine we had done the night before. Prayer time was a joke. I think mine this time was worse than the night before. I made up my mind; the next night, I was going to try praying the way I was imagining Seanna praying.

As we got ready for bed, Jenny and I discussed our day. She kept her description of her day to a minimum, skipping all of the other nurses' dramas she usually talked about when I asked her about her day. I assumed she did this because she could sense there was something bothering me.

When she asked me about my day, I went into the story of our trip to the store. She listened intently and interrupted me with comments as I unfolded the events.

"I should have warned you that today was, 'Shop with a Cop Day.' Some of the gals at work have been talking about it," she said when I told her how crowded it was.

"Why did she pick those things out of all the things in the store?" she wondered. I had to tell her to stop interrupting and to let me finish the story.

"What? You lost her?" she screamed in horror when I came to that part of the story. I thought she was going to smack me. I had to remind her that I still brought her home safe and sound. She finally let me finish the story, I think, only because she was crying too hard to say anything else.

"She is really a special girl. She only had that little boy in mind picking out those gifts. She didn't even think of herself," Jenny said after gathering herself.

"How do you think she knows what note to give and to whom? I mean, you should have seen these men. That note was exactly what they needed to understand, and I have a feeling they truly listened to what it said. Is she just pulling them out of her pocket without understanding what they mean?" I asked her, confused.

"I think she can read," Jenny said thoughtfully.

"No way; she's barely five years old," I protested.

"Some kids read that early."

"Maybe you're right. I suppose when confronted with a handicap you compensate with other talents, but how could a child know how to pick the moment and create that kind of an effect?" I asked, humbly remembering the faces of the three men.

"You mean that kind of an effect on you," she whispered, looking into my eyes. Her eyes were still moist.

"I don't know how to handle this stuff. Have I really been this hard-hearted?" I hung my head. I was feeling ashamed for how I had lived my life these past few years.

"Oh Max," Jenny said, giving me a spouse-comforting hug. We hugged for a while. It felt good, like when I was a child and just needed a hug to cause everything to make sense and be okay. I was confused and had no idea why Seanna was having this effect on me. I did not know if I liked it or not.

We talked for another half an hour. It seemed like we had not had this much to talk about for the last couple of years. There had seemed to be plenty to talk about while we were dating, but once married, our conversations were not so intimate. Lately, our conversations seemed more like the scheduling meeting of a boss with his secretary.

"So, what do you have going on tomorrow?" Jenny would usually ask, and I would then fill her in on the boring details of my next day's activities. The conversations generally did not include much sentiment. These last few nights, though, felt like we were dating again; we just wanted to know everything about what the other one was doing and feeling. Jenny confided that she was glad I had that experience and not her. She was certain she could not have handled it.

"I sure hope the rest of my month doesn't go like this," I said, getting into bed.

"By the way, your dad called again. I don't know why you won't just talk to him."

"I don't know if I can."

"He's been trying to talk to you ever since you quit."

"What can I say after what I did?"

"Well, you'd better figure it out. I invited your parents over Friday night. They want to meet Seanna."

"You did?" Uneasiness filled my body.

"Yes, and they're very excited," she said as if it were the end of the discussion. The tone of her voice was sleepy, so I did not pursue the conversation further. I kissed her good-night, and she fell asleep.

Chapter 5

The next two days were quiet and uneventful. Seanna spent most of her time playing with the toys Jenny had brought home that her friends at work had given her. Seanna loved all of the books they had sent for her, too. Miss Hinder was right. Seanna loved the children's religious books. She loved to lay belly-down on the carpet in front of the Christmas tree, next to the gas fireplace in the front sitting room, slowly turning the pages. She seemed as though she were just looking at the pictures, but once in a while she would point to a word with her little finger. *Jenny might be right. She might be reading after all.* She looked so cute with her bare feet sticking up in the air and crossed at the ankles.

When she was not reading, Seanna was watching a movie in the corner of the main room of the house, which consisted of the kitchen, dining area, and sofa area that had the television on the wall. That first day I had brought her home, she was quite excited to see such a big television hanging there. I was glad she noticed it because it was my only contribution to the decorating of the inside of the house. To me, it looked like a work of art up against the cream paint, a masterpiece which only added to the grandeur of the sports games I loved to watch.

One night Jenny brought home some old classic Christmas movies, which kept Seanna occupied for long periods of time. I just hovered in the kitchen and around the four-chair dining table, which looked awkwardly small in the big space that was designated for the dining area. I was trying to search the papers and Internet for jobs; I was not having much luck. I was completely sick with anxiety about Friday night. I spent almost every minute trying to think of something that I could say to fix my mistake and patch my relationship with my dad. So far, nothing I could think of was going to work, and my parents were coming over the next evening.

I was excited to see them. I had missed my mom very much. She always knew how to help me when she knew there was something that worried me. I remembered the time when I was contemplating marrying Jenny. Was it the right move for me? Mom could always tell when something was wrong and would poke and prod me until I finally told her.

"I just don't know if it's the right thing to do," I told her, finally letting her penetrate my wall.

"Do you love her?" she asked.

"Of course I do, Mom, but…"

"But what? Does anything other than that matter?" she said sternly.

"No, I guess not, but…"

"Then what are you worried about? Do you think she wants to marry you?" she added, cutting me off again.

"I wouldn't have bought the ring if I thought that she didn't. It's just her parents. They don't like me at all, and they seem to voice that around me constantly. So, I know they badger her when she's at home," I said, whining. Jenny, being the oldest child, was expected to marry into wealth so she could help take care of her parents when they wanted to retire. They had done nothing to save up for it. So, they would say anything to Jenny to change her mind about me. "What if she starts to believe what they say, and it ruins our marriage?" I asked, feeling incompetent.

"Is what they're saying true?"

"Absolutely not," I huffed.

"Then, do you think Jenny is stupid?" she asked.

"What?" *Why would she ask that?*

"Look, I love Jenny and am happy that you found such a wonderful girl to marry. You've been dating for a year and a half, and she still keeps coming around," my mom said tenderly.

"Yeah, go figure," I sighed. I still had no idea what Jenny had seen in me. I did not have much to offer.

"Does she know you have the ring?"

"No, I picked it out myself. She doesn't even know I'm thinking marriage yet. It'll be a complete surprise. I don't know. Maybe I'm crazy to think she would even say yes."

"Don't be like that. She's still here because she loves you, and I think she's going to be the happiest woman on earth when you pop that question," she said tenderly. "As for her parents, they are who they are, and just be grateful that Jenny fell far from that tree. Your dad says he doesn't know if he can handle being around them during the wedding without smacking that father of hers."

"Mom!" I said, surprised.

"I know, I know. I need to be more charitable," she laughed. "Now tell me again how you plan on asking her." I began explaining my plans for the proposal. I was going to pretend to have the car break down on the bridge over the river on our way home from one of Jenny's dance competitions. I would then have her walk down under the bridge with me to get some water for the radiator. Giving her a container to fill, hopefully she would then see the big white plastic clam with the ring inside that I would previously have deposited. "A romantic, just like your father," my mother said after helping me fine-tune the details.

That was how it was most of the time with my mom. She always knew how to change the situation around with questions, love, and humor. However, despite her magic, I couldn't help but feel that it might be a big disaster with my father when my parents came to visit the next day.

I seemed to fill my days with thoughts of everything that had gone wrong in my life; these thoughts were only interrupted by tea parties with Seanna under the Christmas tree. Some of the dolls and stuffed animals Jenny had borrowed were our tea party guests, most of which looked like they had been well-loved by their previous owners. Seanna loved playing house in the big closet in her room; she and I thought it was just right for a little girl's house. Still, my favorite activity was reading Seanna some of the books she loved so much.

I must have been totally engulfed in my self-pity, for I never noticed that Seanna had turned the television off and grabbed a book for me to read. She must have been watching me for a while because the look on her face was somber and full of concern. She came and sat next to me on the couch and peered into my eyes; I looked away.

"What book do we have now?" I asked, trying to change my mood. Seanna grabbed my face in her hands the same way that Jenny did when she wanted me to listen or to talk about what was bothering me. I looked into Seanna's speckled brown eyes. I do not know why, but I felt that I should just tell her everything that was bothering me.

"I'm sorry, Seanna. I've been somewhat distant lately. It's just that my dad and mom are coming over, and…." I broke off. She was obviously excited. She smiled her dimply smile and clapped her hands. I had heard Jenny refer to my parents as "Grandpa and Grandma." I supposed that was what made Seanna so excited. Who doesn't like grandparents?

"Well, I did something very bad a couple of years ago that cost my dad dearly, and I'm not sure my dad likes me anymore." *That's as much detail as a five-year-old needs to know,* I thought. There was a distinct lump in the back of my throat now.

"It's just going to be hard to talk to him after I haven't seen him for these past years," I choked. Seanna glanced over to her brown coat on the floor and then back to me. She smiled and gave me a hug. I did not know how, but it made me feel better. Sharing with Seanna gave me a renewed determination to fix my relationship with my dad.

I started to read the book that Seanna had handed me. It was one of the religious books. This one was about Christ and his death. I wondered why God would let the people treat his son the way they did in the events surrounding his death. When we came to the part about the burial of Christ, Seanna got a panicked look on her face and started to point to the picture on the page.

"He died, but the story goes on. After three days he came back to life," I said, watching her reaction. Now I was grateful for those boring Sunday church lessons my mom had made me attend. Seanna was not satisfied though. She tapped the picture of the cave where Jesus was buried, and then pointed to her scar. Panic struck my heart. I did not know much more about that story of Christ, so I did not know what to tell her to comfort her. She shook her head; tears filled her eyes. I was at a loss.

"You're not going to die," I said, confused. She pointed again to her scar.

"You almost did, but you survived." Then it dawned on me. Maybe she wanted to know about her family.

"Are you wondering about your family?" I guessed. She nodded, shedding a tear.

"I don't know much about what happened or where they buried your parents." What a hard thing for a young girl to have to try to understand. I was not sure what else to say. I had not been able to ask any more questions when I picked her up at the orphanage. She was sobbing now; the tiny tears flowed over her cheeks.

"Look. Sharon is supposed to stop by Saturday, so I'll ask her more details when she gets here." Seanna shook her head in a "That won't help" look.

"If she can't tell me anything, then I'll go down to the police station and see if anybody there can help me." I figured that might be a long shot because it would be a Saturday, and they might not be there. Seanna crossed her heart with her tiny hands.

"I promise," I said seriously. That promise seemed to settle her down.

As frustrating as the whole conversation was for me, trying to figure out what Seanna wanted to say without her voice, I was sure it had to be a hundred times worse for her. How frustrating must it be for any person, let alone a little girl, to not be able to communicate verbally? Was that what the rest of her life was going to be like for her?

That evening when Jenny got home, we completed our nightly ritual of dinner, play, bath, stories, and prayers. Prayer time was becoming one of my favorite times of the day. I tried to pray more from the heart now, more like how I imagined Seanna was praying. I think she approved because she was not shaking her head at me as she had before. Jenny was doing the same. It was a beautiful thing to hear her pray. For me it was still a little awkward, but it felt good to talk to God the same way I used to talk to my dad. That night, for a time, I reflected on my last deep conversation with Dad. He was so easy to talk to before my big mistake. Just a couple of days before that day, I had confided in him my feelings about Jenny's infertility situation.

"All I ever wanted to do was to make her happy, and she just isn't. They say it could develop into bigger health problems. I don't know what I would do if anything else should happen to her. I can't even imagine not having her with me," I said, heartbroken at the thought.

"I know what you mean, Son. I don't know what I would do without your mother in my life," my dad said, putting his arm around me. "There are just some times in life when you have to trust in God and believe that He knows what's best for us," he added, stepping lightly.

"I don't know about the whole God thing, Dad. There are just too many unanswered questions," I said, wondering how God could do this to Jenny.

"If they were answered, would you believe then? More than likely, you wouldn't. Sometimes we need to have faith in the things we need before He can help us," Dad said, trying to teach me. He was always a religious person and full of wisdom. "Jenny's a tough girl. She would have to be to put up with you. Why, the toughest girl I know is that way because she raised you," he added, lightening the conversation.

"That's funny. She tells me all the time it's because she has to put up with you," I joked, glad to get away from the previous subject.

Could we ever get those times back, I wondered, *or did I ruin it for life?*

As Jenny and I were getting ready for bed, I related the whole conversation that Seanna and I had that afternoon.

"What are you going to do?" she said with a concerned look on her face.

"Well, I promised her I would go to the station, and if it comes to that, I will."

"But if you do find something out, and it's not good, what will you tell her?"

"The truth, because I know that's what she wants," I said, determined.

That was as far as the conversation went because Jenny was so tired. She managed to mumble, just before falling asleep, "Remember, your parents will be here at five o'clock tomorrow."

At least that was one good thing about the conversation with Seanna. It had kept me from thinking about what was coming the next day. As I thought about it, I did not seem to have the same worry as before. My situation did not hold a candle to Seanna's loss. I was just going to face my dad and deal with whatever came. Things certainly could not get any worse in our relationship. I did not even want to think about it anymore. My focus now was on how I was going to keep my promise to that little girl sleeping across the hall.

Friday passed by way too fast. It was soon three o'clock, and I was extremely nervous. How did the day pass so quickly? I had gotten up early with Seanna, something I looked forward to doing every morning. She was the best alarm clock I had ever had. We played our usual morning games after breakfast. She did not want to watch movies, which was out of the ordinary. Instead, she helped me clean the house for the guests coming that night a task that I was sure I could have done a lot faster by myself, but she insisted. She finally fell asleep for her nap. It was clear that Seanna had kept me very busy throughout the day.

Was that part of the secret that Jenny and Seanna had shared the night before? Jenny had joked to Seanna, just before leaving for work, something about their plan they had figured out the previous night. Maybe it was to keep me so busy that I would not have time to think about seeing my dad again. If it was, then it worked out perfectly. Seanna had carried out her orders down to the last bat of her tired eyes, with a preciseness of which any general would be proud. That would also explain all of the phone calls from Jenny giving me more stuff to finish before she got home. *That's not fair! They're scheming against me!* I thought, frustrated.

"So, you plotted against me. I can't believe you made the little one do all the work," I said, taking Jenny by surprise as she walked in the door.

"What?" she said, giving me the "deer in the headlight" look.

"Yeah, well, it worked. She kept me so busy that I just realized that my parents will be here in less than an hour."

"It worked then! Wonderful! I was hoping she could hold out until I made it home."

"You're ruthless," I said, scooping her into my arms, dipping her down as if we were dancing, and kissing her.

"I know, but it's for your own good," she teased.

I was amazed at how much our relationship had improved over the last week. We were in love again. It wasn't that we had not loved each other before, but the flame was definitely being starved for oxygen. I did not know how, but I knew that Seanna was definitely helping us get that flame back. Whatever it was, I was determined to keep it going because it was great. The flame was hotter than ever.

"You're home early, and Seanna is sleeping," I said lustfully, still holding Jenny parallel to the floor. .

"Ooo, are you suggesting something?" she flirted back.

"Yes. I was thinking about my dad, and I need you to take my mind off it."

"How can I help?"

"Well you could......" I trailed off as I heard the "Sss, sss, sss, sss" behind us. I almost dropped Jenny on the ground, but she jumped straight up instead. Her face was flushed with embarrassment.

"We need to start cooking dinner. Everybody to the kitchen!" Jenny giggled as she regained her balance. I was pretty sure I was about as red as the shirt I had on when I reached the kitchen. Jenny and Seanna had already started getting things out to cook dinner. Jenny just smiled at me, blushing.

The doorbell rang in what seemed like just minutes later. My heart raced. The moment had arrived.

"I can do this," I mumbled to myself. As I left the kitchen to get the door, I glanced back at Jenny and Seanna. The expressions on their faces were those of encouragement, but it did not help. I opened the door, and my mom burst through, giving me a giant bear hug.

"My long, lost son," she raved.

"Hi, Mom. It's good to see you," I said with the only breath that was not squeezed out of me.

"Where is that beautiful wife of yours?" she replied.

"Hello, Lacy, how are you?" Jenny said, coming out of the kitchen to give her a hug.

"I'm better now that we're here with you two again. Thank you for putting this together. It's gone on long enough," she said gratefully.

"I agree," said Jenny. I had a hunch that Jenny had set all this up, and hearing those words my suspicions were confirmed.

"And, who is this little pearl?" My mother had barely noticed Seanna standing shyly by the kitchen entryway. Seanna needed no invitation; she ran to my mom and gave her a hug. Mom was ecstatic. I think her greatest goal in life was to be a grandma. I guessed this was as close to that as she might get, considering I'm an only child, and Jenny and I are unable to have children of our own. That news had almost done my mother in. Jenny had said that Mom took it almost as badly as she did.

As the women fussed over the little girl, I turned my attention back outside, looking for my dad. He was getting some things out of the trunk. He came to the door carrying some presents. When he reached the front porch, our eyes met. His expression was one of loving concern, not the one of anger and disappointment that I had expected.

"Hi, Max," he said formally.

"Hi, Jim," I replied, and we shook hands. That was it. He slid past me, placed the presents under the Christmas tree, and joined the girls in the kitchen.

The presents looked odd under the tree. They were the only ones there. It reminded me that I still had no idea what I was going to get for Seanna. At least I did not have to worry about Jenny this year. We had decided that we were not going to get gifts for each other, just Seanna. That would help the money we had budgeted for Christmas to go a little further.

Was that it then? Just like that, it was over with my dad. It reminded me of the time I got into a fistfight with my best friend in high school over a girl whom we both wanted to date. After beating each other up, we were best friends again the next day. We both had fat lips and scars, but it made for some funny stories for the guys. It turned out that the girl did not want to date either one of us. *Is it really going to be that easy?* I was still skeptical.

"I forgot what a great cook you married," Mom said.

"I sure did," I said, shooting a brownie-point look to Jenny. She smiled back. Seanna just rubbed her stomach.

"Even better than my Mac & Cheese," I said defiantly, looking at her. Seanna thought for a minute and then nodded her head, "Yes."

"Well, at least she had to think about it," I teased. All in all, everything was normal except the lack of conversation between my dad and me. Before the work fiasco, Dad and I would have been in deep discussions of sports, politics, and business. I had missed those dinner conversations. *Perhaps we've grown too much apart to be able to have that again.* That realization made my heart ache.

Seanna was getting all of the attention she wanted and loving it. My parents were great with her. So far, I was the only person that struggled with her not being able to talk, even though I was better at it now than in my first couple of days with her. My mom, dad, and Jenny never seemed to give it much thought, and communication came with ease.

"Jim, did you get all of the presents out of the trunk?" my mom said to my dad when we were all finished eating.

"You're not leaving yet?" Jenny pleaded. Seanna grabbed my dad's arm in a death grip.

"Is it okay if we stay a little longer?" my dad asked, looking straight at me. Seanna flashed me a puppy dog look. All eyes were on me now.

"Sure, but you don't need my permission. We're glad to have you," I answered. Seanna clapped her hands.

"Then I'll go get the presents and be right back," Dad said to Seanna. Jenny nodded at me to go help him. I knew what that meant. It was time that he and I dealt with each other. I got up and put on my coat. As I opened the door and went outside, I could hear the girls cleaning up dinner. I met my dad at the trunk of his car.

"Dad," I said, shuddering.

"Yes, Son," he said as if he had been waiting for this moment. My mind went blank, and I froze. I'm not sure how long I stood there like an idiot. It seemed like forever. It was certainly long enough for Seanna to run out of the house in her brown coat, slide in between us, facing my dad, and give him a note.

"Forgive," he read aloud. He bent down on one knee and gave her a hug. "I think this is a very appropriate note for this situation," he said as his eyes began to moisten up.

I suddenly took courage in having Seanna there. "I'm sorry, Dad. I never meant to hurt you or your business. When I made that mistake, I just got careless and lost my cool. I'm sorry I cost you your best client…"

"Max!" he interrupted me. "You didn't do anything that I wouldn't have done myself. Truth is…that company, even though they bought the most from us, was not our best client, not by a long shot. They were a pain in the butt from day one. I'm surprised I let it go that long, and, honestly, I was trying to think of a way to get rid of them. Business was starting to suffer for the other, more reliable, clients. Although I wasn't going to go about it the way you did, it worked out just the same."

"Why didn't you tell me?"

"What do you think I've been trying to do for the last two years?" I suddenly felt guilty for not returning any of the calls from him. My stupid pride got in the way.

"I thought you just wanted to let me know how frustrated you were with me," I admitted.

"The only thing I was frustrated about was how you were handling it all and avoiding me. I thought I had raised a man, not a mouse," he explained. These words hurt, but they were true. I had run instead of standing up and facing the music. I suddenly felt sick. I had wasted two years of precious time; I could never get that back, and it was all over a client that my dad had wanted to get rid of anyway.

"I'm sorry, Dad. I thought you were so upset with me. I just couldn't face you."

"Look, even if they were the lifeline of the business, no client, or any business for that matter, is worth losing a son over." It was obvious that he had been hurting just as much as I had over the lost relationship. I felt even guiltier.

"Dad, I'm so sor....."

"I forgive you. Now can we get back to how it used to be?"

"I would like that very much," I said, relieved.

"Now, hug me so that your wife, and mine, will know we made up." I looked up at the front window just as the blinds snapped shut. The girls had been spying on us. I hugged my dad.

"I love you, Son."

"I love you too, Dad."

"Now, shall we go inside and open some of these presents?" he said, looking at Seanna, who had a big look of relief on her face. It turned into a big "You bet" grin.

The rest of the evening was just like old times. We talked over dessert and all had a good time. We were a family again. Seanna loved all of her gifts. I finally realized how much I had missed my dad and mom. I thought I was happy before, but having them back in my life again was so rewarding. It filled the void that was a lot bigger than I had previously thought. I was even sad to see them go. Seanna was, too. She had my dad in that death grip again as he started to get up to get his coat, so I invited them back for Christmas Eve and Christmas Day. Seanna let go of him only after my parents had crossed their hearts that they would come and spend the night on Christmas Eve.

Chapter 6

I woke up to a sound that was becoming a favorite of mine: the music of little slippers that were scooting cautiously down the hall and stopping at my door. I raised my head and looked over at Seanna.

"I'm coming, Seanna," I said sleepily, but joyfully.

"No! You stay in bed, Max. It's my turn for morning duty," Jenny said happily.

"Are you sure?" I said, surprised.

"Yes! You can't have all the fun," she joked defiantly. As I looked at Seanna, she almost seemed to have a disappointed look on her face as she saw Jenny get out of bed instead of me.

I heard the girls in the kitchen getting breakfast, and it dawned on me that the evening before had been so pleasant that I had forgotten what day it was. It was Saturday, and Jenny had the day off. I had a day to do whatever I wanted without my five-year-old escort. I suddenly felt a wave of guilt run through my body. *What was that all about?* I thought in a panic. *Why should I feel guilty about having some alone time for just me?* I tried to shake the feeling, but it would not go away. I fought with myself for a couple of minutes, and then I gave up. The truth was that I actually did not want alone time. Really, all I wanted to do was to be with my beautiful wife and our holiday guest. I jumped out of bed and started getting ready for the day. I did not want to miss one more minute with them.

I felt different. If I had to describe the feeling, it would be that I felt lighter: lighter, as though a burden had been lifted off my shoulders. I smiled when I thought of the huge misunderstanding that had taken so much precious time from being with my parents. *I sure am glad that we made it through, and the darkness is gone.*

Despite feeling as if I were floating, I also had a feeling that I was forgetting something I was supposed to do that day. *It must be something important because I feel sick thinking about it.* I wondered to myself what it could be and was beginning to panic. I retraced the events of the day before in my mind. I had not committed to anything for my mom, dad, or Jenny. Had I? I thought of the dinner, the talk with my dad, and the rest of the evening. Then, it hit me as I remembered my parents promising to come for Christmas Eve and to stay overnight for Christmas. I had crossed my heart, just as they had done, sealing a promise to Seanna. I was going to find out all I could about her family and what happened to them.

"I can't believe I almost forgot about my promise," I muttered angrily to myself. Seanna had only been with us for a short while, but she had blessed my life so much and taught me things in a way no one else could. How could I go and forget one of the only things she had asked for since I picked her up? I could not let her down. I was determined to keep my promise to her and was very grateful that I had remembered my promise before it was too late.

As we finished cleaning up a delightful breakfast, the doorbell rang.

"The staff member," we said together. Seanna looked at me and crossed her heart. I shook my head in an understanding gesture. She had not forgotten my promise.

"That's right," Jenny said, catching on. Then, quick like a racehorse, Seanna galloped from the room and threw open the front door.

"Hello, Seanna," Sharon said happily. Seanna gave her a big hug. "I miss you, too."

"How are you, Sharon?" I asked, putting forth my hand.

"I'm well, Mr. Fox, and this must be your wife," she said, shaking my hand and then Jenny's.

"You can call me Max. Please come in. Yes, this is my wife, Jenny. Jenny, Sharon."

"Won't you sit down, please?" Jenny said in a formal voice.

Sharon stayed for about an hour. Despite the pleasant, friendly conversation we had, it was just as I thought; Sharon had no idea about what had happened to the remains of Seanna's parents.

"They don't like to tell us much about the children's past lives. They think it will change the way we act and work around them. We only know so much about Seanna because of the scar, and we have told you everything we know," she said, looking at me sadly when I asked her about Seanna's family. She did confirm, however, my idea about going to the police station and seeing if they had any information.

Sharon went with Seanna to look at her room and to talk to her alone for a while, probably to find out if we were treating her okay. It made me nervous. What was Seanna telling her? I was the one spending the most time with her, so if the report was bad, then I was to blame.

Finally, it was our turn to be interrogated. "Seanna tells me that she is very happy here," Sharon reported while sitting with us in the kitchen. "That's shocking for me to believe after the way Max acted the day he picked her up," she said, laughing. Then, she asked us several questions to make sure we were treating Seanna the way we should be. Jenny did most of the talking. I was preoccupied, trying to figure out how to find the answers to Seanna's questions about her parents.

"I guess we passed," I said to Seanna as Sharon drove away. "You're still here. Thanks for not telling her how mean I am," I whispered to her in a secretive way.

"Sss, sss, sss," Seanna laughed.

"That was pleasant, wasn't it?" Jenny said. Seanna drew a heart on her chest and then pointed after Sharon.

"I like her too," Jenny said. Seanna looked at me with that dimply grin. I knew what it meant.

"Yes, I know," I said, concerned. "I'll go to the police station right now to see what I can find out." What if I couldn't find any new information, or what if the information I did find was horrible? I did not want to disappoint or hurt Seanna. I suddenly felt as though this were going to be the hardest thing I had ever done. Seanna and Jenny must have read the expression on my face because they both hugged me at the same time to comfort me.

I pulled up to the station, and my heart sank. Closed. This was just as I had expected on a Saturday. Yet, I knew that I could not go back home without finding someone to help me. The thought of the disappointment on Seanna's face made me feel like crying. The day she made me promise to do this for her was still stuck in my mind. She was so worried about her parents' bodies. I sat in the car for ten minutes in front of the station, thinking of that conversation with her. I don't know why. What was I expecting? Was somebody just going to drive up and help me? I think it was the fear of going home empty-handed that kept me there. Finally, I did not know what else to do, so sadly I began to put the car in reverse. Then, I got a crazy idea. Maybe saying a prayer might help. The teachers during those Sunday school lessons always said to pray when we needed help. I had been practicing at night with the girls and on my own, too, after Jenny had fallen asleep. If ever I needed some divine help, it was now. I put the car in park again, and feeling a little funny, I started to pray aloud.

"Dear Father," I stuttered humbly. "I know I am new to this, and who knows if I am doing it right? First, I would like to thank You for letting me get to know Seanna. She is teaching me so much about having faith. Thank You so much for helping my dad and me heal our relationship. Father, I now need Your help. I know that I am unworthy, but Seanna has been such an angel, even with all that she has endured in life. If ever there were a person who deserved a blessing, it is her. I am trying to help her. I feel lost as to what to do. Forgive me for my helplessness. Will You help me find out about Seanna's parents? I know You are busy, and I am just one of many who plead for Your help. Oh, Father, please help me, please. I have not done much right in my life, but thanks to Seanna, I am trying harder now. Please help me. I love You. In Jesus' name I pray, Amen."

I waited, sitting in the car for ten more minutes, but still nothing happened. What was I expecting? Was I to see a vision, or what? Then I saw the cop car in the rearview mirror. My heart raced excitedly. At least now I could say I talked to someone, even if he were not able to help me. Maybe he could point me in the right direction. I could not help but feel grateful; it felt like an answer to my prayer.

"Can I help you, Sir?" the officer said, rolling down his window as I approached his car.

"Yes Officer. I'm looking for some information on a car accident that happened about this time last year," I said hopefully.

"Son, it's the beginning of winter. Do you know how many accidents happen this time of year?" he said half-jokingly. Despite the respect that his uniform demanded, he was a very jolly man, about in his late fifties. He reminded me of my grandpa by the way he smiled but tried to be serious at the same time.

"I guess there would be, with all the snow we have. I think, though, this accident would be different than most."

"Well, describe it to me, and I'll see if I can help," he said, getting out of his car. "I deal with most of the accident reports, being Sheriff and all, so there is a good chance that I can help you."

"Oh, I'm sorry. I didn't know you were the sheriff."

"That's okay. Let's go inside and out of the cold. You're lucky to have caught me here. I usually don't come to the office on Saturday. I actually don't even work on Saturday. I just happen to be filling in for one of the other officers today, and I had forgotten something in my office, so I came to pick it up."

"I'll take it as a real blessing then, Sheriff."

"Well, let's see if I can help you first," he said, sitting behind his desk. He motioned for me to sit down. "When did you say the accident happened?" he started.

"It was about this time last year. It was a bad accident where two people died, but a little girl lived. She would have been four years old at the time." At that moment, his joyful demeanor changed to one of heartbroken sadness. I did not say any more after seeing his mood change. He spoke again after about thirty seconds of silence.

"Yeah, I remember that accident. Poor Seanna. The cutest little girl I ever saw. What an ordeal she has been through."

"You know Seanna then?" I asked, knowing his answer.

"I tell you, son, I've been dealing with accidents like this for thirty years, and I never saw such a sight in my life. By the time I arrived on scene, there wasn't much left of the car or the family. Just a very badly burned sixteen-year-old and Seanna."

"Did the boy live?" I asked.

"Barely. He was burned over seventy percent of his body. He managed to keep the girl from being burned, not an easy thing to do when a car explodes right next to you. Robert Doss was the boy's name. His family had just moved here. Really nice folks, the Dosses are. They had only been here two weeks when the boy witnessed the accident. He was on his way home, driving behind a semi that went out of control when it hit a snowdrift that had blown onto the road. The semi slid into the oncoming lane and hit Seanna's car head-on. They never really had a chance in that little four-door car. Robert jumped out and ran to the car even though it was on fire. Brave boy, I tell you. He saved Seanna's life. She would have burned-up with her parents had he not pulled her out."

The sheriff looked down at his desk for a couple of seconds, pondering the scene in his mind.

"I'm afraid Robert's heroic act has scarred him for life. He'll never be the same again. He's had surgery after surgery, but he still doesn't look right. The kids at school don't know what he did, or they don't care, because he is the victim of a lot of jokes and pranks. I had gotten to know him really well while I was investigating the accident. He still stops by occasionally to see me. I don't think he has a friend in town, being a new kid and looking the way he does. It's good he has such a good family, or I'm afraid he would have called it quits by now. I'll never forget the scene when I pulled up to the car, which was half melted, and Seanna and Robert were lying in the snow twenty feet away. I thought they were dead, too. It was a miracle that either Robert or Seanna lived. Of course, Seanna wasn't left without a scar either. She wasn't burned, but her throat collapsed, and as I understand, she was left unable to talk. The cutest little dimply smile you ever did see though," he said, regaining his jolliness.

"I know," I said, shaking the accident scene from my mind.

"How do you know Seanna? What's your interest in her accident?" he asked, confused.

"It's a long story, but my wife and I adopted her for the holidays from the orphanage. Seanna wanted me to find out about what happened to her parents' bodies." The sheriff turned somber again.

"Well, they were laid to rest out in the new cemetery west of town. I believe they're in the northeast corner. You can't miss them; they're the barest headstones out there. You know, I still can't figure out how two people with a little family can go missing, and no one would come looking for them. I realize they could have been lost, but still, somebody should be missing them and sending out a report on them. After ten months of searching and sending out missing person reports, with not even one response, I was forced to give up." He looked devastated. "I was really hoping to get Seanna home to some grandparents or some other family member for this Christmas since last Christmas she was in the hospital the whole time." Then his face changed as he said happily, "How is Seanna?"

"She's good. She can't talk, but those dimples make up for it. She's really good at getting her thoughts across to you, though," I said, smiling. The sheriff laughed.

"I bet she does. I heard she's very smart. I'm glad to see she's found a good family to be with for the holiday," he said as he stood up from the desk. "Is there anything else that I can help you with, Mr…?"

"Max" I said, standing up. "You can call me Max. And no, I don't have any more questions now, but thank you for your help."

"Well, I'm glad to have helped. Anything I can do for Seanna is my privilege. I do have a favor to ask of you, Max." He looked directly into my eyes for a response. "Will you take Seanna to visit Robert? He asks me about her every time I talk to him. I think he wants to see her, but he's a little embarrassed about his looks, and he's afraid that he'll scare her. I think it might do him some good to see her again; you know, lift his spirits a little to see the girl he saved."

"I would love to meet him myself. Where can I find him, Sheriff?"

"Call me Neal. I think the best place would be to catch him as he's getting out of school," he said as we walked to our cars.

"How will I know who he is?" I asked.

"Trust me, you'll know," he sighed, getting back into his patrol car.

"Thank you, Sheriff Neal."

"Let me know if I can help you with anything else. Sorry to cut this short, but I have to go. Promise me though; you will take Seanna to see Robert."

"I promise and thanks again." He put the car in reverse and drove away.

During dinner, I related everything about my adventure to the girls. When I told them about my prayer, and the miracle that happened, Seanna clapped reverently to let me know I had done the right thing. Jenny just looked at me, shocked, as though she did not realize I had it in me. Then, I told them about what I had learned from Sheriff Neal, minus the gory details about the accident. I was worried about how Seanna would take the news, but she acted very excited to have found out what happened to her parents' bodies. I suppose that could add some closure to a child's mind. Seanna made me cross my heart on the promise to take her to see Robert. I was unsure if that was a good idea, but once again, I made a promise, so not following through was not an option.

The next morning I awoke to a lovely little girl standing in my doorway wearing her Sunday dress. I could not help waking Jenny to show her how pretty Seanna looked.

"Do you think she's expecting us to take her to church?" I asked after we made a fuss over her.

"I think that's exactly what she wants, and it is Sunday," Jenny sighed. This was going to be difficult. We had not been to a church for years. The thought of it made me want to tell Seanna no, but I held my tongue.

"I suppose we could go to the one we drive by almost every day," I suggested.

"What religion goes to that church?" she asked.

"I have no idea."

"Oh, this is going to be good," she laughed.

"What church do you think she's used to attending?" I asked, not really expecting a response. It was not as if Jenny were going to know that. She just gave me a shrug. I already felt embarrassed about going to church and I had not even gotten out of bed yet. I think the hardest thing to face was that I was certain that Seanna knew more about religion than I did. How was I supposed to act as if I had been doing this for my whole life?

After eating breakfast and getting ready, we went to the little church on the corner. Jenny made some phone calls and found out that the meeting started at 9:00 am. I was glad for that; we would still have the rest of the day to do fun activities as a family. We pulled into the parking lot and parked the car. I think Seanna sensed that we were faking our enthusiasm about going to church when neither one of us opened a door to get out of the car. She leaned forward in her car seat and pointed to the door handle on Jenny's side of the car, as if we had no idea how to open it. I laughed. Seanna was excited. I wondered if she had been to this church before.

"Well, here we go, ready or not," I exclaimed, trying to fake my excitement. Walking up to the church, I could not help but notice how awesome it looked. Being in a newer part of the suburbs, it had not been here long-maybe one or two years. It had a sleek modern design, with pillars lining the front entrance near the main door. The structure on the roof directly over the main doors was long and about half as wide as its length. The pillars seemed to point right toward it. I think it was some sort of a spire, or steeple, pointing upward. The entire church was made of white brick with dark-colored grout. At the entrance, we were greeted by a man who seemed to be very important although he was not wearing anything to signify he was different from anybody else who was coming or going from the church. A white shirt with a tie was the norm, which made things worse for me because I had chosen to wear a black shirt and no tie. Jenny and Seanna fit right in, though, with the dresses they wore. The greeter was an older man, tall in stature and balding. He was very friendly but had the handshake of a crocodile bite. He acted very interested in Seanna and in us.

I felt very uncomfortable, and I could tell Jenny did, too. Seanna, however, trotted around the place as if she were at home. She shook everyone's hand and smiled; nobody seemed to know her, so I figured she had not been there before. Still, she had a glow about her, brighter than I had ever seen. After the door greeter interrogated us, he led us to a place to sit. The way he fussed over us, he might as well have yelled to everybody in the congregation that we were new and here for the first time. I was glad to finally sit down in the back. Then, I could just sink into the bench and hide.

The room we were in was longer than it was wide, fitting the contour of the roofline outside. I noticed that the hallway we passed down to get to the room was lined with doors to what looked like some classrooms. The main room had long benches lining the middle of it, with smaller ones on the edges, leaving two pathways in between. The carpet was commercial grade; it was dark green with specks in it, giving it the look of a mossy stream. At the front of the room was a podium, which I assumed was for the preacher. I glanced over at Jenny, who was looking very uncomfortable. She seemed like she wanted to make a run for the outside door.

"You can probably make it before that door greeter sees you," I laughed.

"Yes, but if he catches me, then he'll interrogate me again. I don't want to go through that again. I'll take my chances sitting right here," she said seriously. Seanna hissed, clearly amused by our behavior.

I have to admit, the meeting was not that bad. I actually felt good about being there after my nerves calmed down.

When it was over, though, the greeter told us about the "other" meeting that was about to start. This one we could go to as a couple, but then there would be another one where we would all be separated. We tried to make up some excuse to get out of the meetings, but he acted as if he had heard them all before and saw right through us. Seanna disappeared with a little girl who had been sitting in front of us. The girl seemed to know where to go. The little girl's mother told us where they were going when she saw the worried expression on Jenny's face. Jenny was not satisfied until the mother took us to see where the children were meeting. After assessing the situation and finding no harm, we consented to go where they directed us. Several other people joined the greeter in herding us to the next class. It felt like we were sheep being funneled into the sheering pin.

In the end, I did not even mind that our church outing was three hours long. I laughed as I thought of how Jenny was pried away from my arm during the third hour of class so that she could go with all the females and I with all the males. It was hard to tell who was hanging on tighter, her or me, because I did not want to be left alone either.

Jenny looked radiant as we walked back to the car. I think she must have liked the experience.

"That was very enjoyable," she said as we got into the car.

"See, nothing to be afraid of," I said. Seanna hissed and rolled her eyes. Then she pointed at me and made a petrified face as if to say, "You were scared to death."

"What are you pointing at? I wasn't afraid. I was cool," I smirked.

"Whatever. I thought you were going to hit the door greeter and run when he started asking where we lived," Jenny laughed. We laughed and joked all the way home. Thankfully, though, it was only an experience that I had to go through once a year. Who knew if we would ever go back? This was just something people did for the Christmas season.

After we ate lunch, Seanna showed us a picture in one of her favorite books. It was the same picture she had used to tell me that she wanted to know about her parents.

"You want to go see your parents' grave sites?" Jenny guessed by her behavior. Seanna flinched at the words "grave sites."

"I don't think that's a good idea," I protested. Seanna put her hands together in a praying motion and pleaded with me.

"I don't know. Are you sure you can handle it?" I asked carefully.

"Are you worried about her, or you?" Jenny asked, looking into my eyes. I felt a lump in my throat.

"What if I'm worried about you?" I whispered. She looked away. I had a feeling this was going to be hard on all of us.

Knowing that we did not have much of a choice, we grabbed our coats and headed to the car. I started the car, and we were off to the cemetery. Nobody said much while we drove there, but it was only an hour from our home. It felt a lot longer than that, though, when we finally pulled into the well-maintained cemetery surrounded by a wrought iron fence. I was not much for cemeteries, not that they scared me; it was just that the only memories I had of them were of my grandparents' burials-not very happy memories. The cemetery was large and kept very clean. In the center there was a large circular pavilion, probably where they held funerals. Someone had been buried there recently; I could tell by the mound of fresh dirt and the uncovered lawn where the snow had been pushed away for those attending. By the amount of footprints, it had just been a small crowd that had gathered. The snow on the ground gave a peaceful atmosphere, muffling the sound of our steps as we walked through the gate. The headstones popped out everywhere in sections, separated by snow-covered paths and lined with barren, leafless trees. As we passed an older section of headstones, I could tell that I was not the only one who did not like cemeteries. Jenny was clinging to my arm for protection, and Seanna had a death grip on Jenny's. We were the only people there, probably because visiting the cemetery is not usually a winter activity unless there is a funeral.

We finally found the area where Seanna's parents were supposedly buried. We had only been searching for the headstone a few minutes when it dawned on me; I had no idea what we were even looking for. I knew it would look new, which helped, but we had no names, so what could be on the headstones? Did they even have headstones, or were they plaques? I suddenly felt horrible for not paying more attention to the details the sheriff gave me. I would hate to take Seanna home disappointed. There were at least six inches of snow, a blanket of snow covering any markers and plaques. It could take hours to find the headstones, and it was too cold to stay outside for long. I again said a small prayer for some help.

I was getting good at this praying thing, and I had a feeling I was not the only one praying. Jenny was standing still, with her eyes closed. She looked like she was in some sort of deep meditation. When she opened her eyes she looked at me, smiling, and then she turned and sprinted in the opposite direction. I yelled at her.

"The sheriff said they were in this section, not that one." Seanna set off after her. *What are they doing?* I quickly ran after them.

When I caught up with them, I could see Jenny standing still, not moving a muscle. In front of a nearly bare headstone, Seanna was kneeling down, holding a note in her hand. I moved to the side to read the words carved into the stone. "The parents of Seanna died November 20, 2010."

Seanna placed a note at the bottom of the gravesite. She was crying. The tears did not look right on her face; she was normally so happy. I guess even the happiest people have to shed a tear at times. Jenny was sobbing uncontrollably. I moved toward her to comfort her, and the lump had moved back into my throat. Jenny buried her face into my shoulder. I was right; this was not a good idea. Seanna straightened the note and started a voiceless wailing. At that moment, I was sure the angels in heaven were crying with her; they would not let one of their own grieve alone. I shuffled Jenny up to the grave, then bent down and picked Seanna up into my arms and hugged her. What else could I do? I have never been very good at this crying, broken heart stuff.

I read the note through my blurred vision and choked when I read the words "Together Forever." I wanted to do something. I wanted to take all of Seanna's pain from her, somehow, even if that meant I had to suffer for the rest of my life without a day of rest. I would do it; I would.

Suddenly, Seanna jumped down and started digging furiously in the snow next to the grave.

"What's wrong? Did you drop something?" I somehow managed to say.

"What is it, honey?" Jenny sobbed. I let go of Jenny and started helping Seanna dig. I was unsure of what I was looking for, but I dug all the way to the other side of the headstone. Then, I found what she was searching for. I could not believe what I saw. It was another marker, a small plaque with the words "Seanna's Baby Brother." No one we had talked to had mentioned a baby brother. Seanna slid into my arms, with Jenny close behind. This was too much. How could a child bear so much pain?

"Please, Lord, what can I do for her?" I prayed aloud. "Tell me anything, please."

We only spent a few more minutes in the cemetery, until Seanna stood up and gave me a "Let's go" look. That was the only signal I needed. The ride home was faster than the ride there even though nobody spoke a word. It was getting late, and Seanna was slumped in her car seat, fast asleep. I wondered if Seanna had been worrying about her brother this whole time; maybe she had not known what had happened to him. Surely somebody would have told her about him. Could she have been left just to wonder about his fate? That must have been eating her up inside.

After carrying the sleeping child in to her bed and closing the door, Jenny mentioned that we had not had any dinner, but there was no way that I was going to wake Seanna up. She had found enough comfort to drift off to sleep, so dinner did not seem as important. I did not feel much like eating either, but Jenny said she was sick to her stomach and needed to eat something. "You've been feeling that way a lot lately," I commented.

"I know. I've scheduled a doctor's appointment for Thursday to see what's going on. So, remember that I'll be coming home late that day," she said in a comforting tone. Not wanting to think of the next week, or of what could be ailing Jenny, I changed the subject.

"How did you know where the grave site was?" I asked her when she sat down to eat.

"Well, I tried your trick. I prayed that I could be a part of a miracle for Seanna. Today in church, when we split into classes, our lesson was on how God is a God of miracles, big and small. I just didn't want to have Seanna be disappointed. It was really strange. After I prayed, I saw the exact location of the headstone in my mind. I even knew what it said before I found it. I think God answered me."

"It only took you a couple of seconds for your miracle to come. I had to wait ten or so minutes for the sheriff to come for mine. That's not fair," I protested.

"You'll have to keep practicing," she joked. "Besides, a miracle is a miracle no matter how long it takes," she added in a spiritual tone.

"Yeah, well, I still haven't received my note from Seanna either," I said, disappointed.

"How do you think she decides who gets one and what note they get?" Jenny asked.

"I haven't figured that out yet. If I had, then I would have five or six notes from her. Instead, I haven't received even one," I huffed grumpily.

"Talk about a miracle: that little girl is one big miracle, and we've been given the gift of taking care of her," Jenny said as we passed by Seanna's bedroom door, looking in at her sleeping peacefully.

"I sure hope there will be more miracles to come," I wished.

"I think we've had lots of miracles granted to us in our lives. We just haven't recognized them," Jenny said thoughtfully as we went into our room.

As I lay in bed, trying to get to sleep, I realized Jenny was right. We had received many small miracles in our lives. How could I have not seen them for what they were? And what was so different in my life that now I could recognize them? I felt different. It was a good type of different, and I did not ever want to go back to how it was before. Everything just seemed clearer, brighter, and better. Life seemed fuller. Not much had changed in my economic situation, but for some reason, that was not as devastating to me, and my hope and self-worth was growing. *Well, whatever is going on, I don't want it to change.*

Chapter 7

It was about five o'clock in the morning when I heard Seanna outside our door. "Why so early?" I mumbled to myself. Then it hit me; my gut felt like it was eating me from the inside out. Seanna was probably starving too; neither of us had eaten anything before bed the night before. I quietly slipped out of bed to make us both something to eat.

Seanna did not seem to be fazed much by how things had turned out at the cemetery. Perhaps that visit to the cemetery had given her all the closure a five-year-old needed. I thought of how nobody had told us about her baby brother. Could it have been that nobody had known? I wanted to find out more about the accident and the investigation.

Seanna wanted to play our usual games, and she was laughing again. I was glad. I liked to see her happy. The brightness just seemed to emanate from her. She had only been with us for a short while, but it seemed like a lot longer. I was more comfortable around her, and I could tell that she did not think I was such a gruff anymore. It was actually fun to spend time with her, and I wanted to spend all the time I could with her. I wanted to know everything about Seanna.

It was funny how my self-pity and selfishness had faded away once she came into my life. There was more to life than my own trials. My thoughts were not focused on me anymore; they were preoccupied with this ball of life sitting next to me, who had already gone through more in her short life than I had in mine. I had never known what it was like to lose somebody that close to me.

Now, if only Seanna would want to go back to bed, then I could go and snuggle with Jenny until the alarm went off. I could tell *that* was not going to happen though. There was absolutely no sleep left in Seanna's eyes. She was ready to start her day.

It was snowing again, which meant it was a little warmer outside. After Jenny left for work, I dressed Seanna up in her hand-me-down snowsuit, and we went outside to make a snowman. It seemed like this was the first time that Seanna had played in snow. She absolutely loved it, and so did I. We tried to make three snowmen that resembled the three of us and, for the most part, they did.

Seanna especially liked having snowball fights and eating the snow. I could only get her to go inside long enough to eat lunch and use the bathroom. We stayed outside all day long. Just before Jenny got home, it started getting colder. We were both wet to the bone, so Jenny came home to find us both warming up in front of the fireplace in the front room. Finding our wet clothes and boots by the garage door, she knew exactly what we had been doing all day.

"Did you have fun in the snow, Seanna?" Jenny asked. Seanna made the motion of throwing a snowball at me and hissed.

"Did you get him good?" Jenny asked, laughing. Seanna nodded, "Yes."

"Hey, you cheat, you're too sneaky," I said, making an excuse.

"Maybe tomorrow you and Max can go sledding," Jenny said happily. Seanna had a fit; she was so excited at those words. I'm sure she had never been sledding before either. For the rest of the evening, she would not let me forget what we were going to do in the morning.

The next day, I took Seanna to the hill just to the north of our house. I had heard some people say that it was a great sledding hill. I had not been sledding since I was a kid. I was almost as excited as Seanna was, and the hill looked better than anything I ever went down in my youth. Of course, Seanna would not go down the hill unless I was with her on the sled. It was a little fast for her to go down alone. At the bottom of the hill, a neighborhood kid had built a jump; neither Seanna nor I felt it was a good run unless we made the jump, and we did it just about every run.

After about two and a half hours, I was exhausted from walking up and down the hill carrying the sled and Seanna. My spinal cord felt like it was compressed to half its size from hitting the jump over and over again, and my stomach hurt from laughing.

Seanna fell asleep within the first minute of the ride home. Luckily, I had followed Jenny's advice and packed some peanut butter and jelly sandwiches and had managed to get one in her before we left the hill. When we arrived home, I carried Seanna into her room and laid her in her bed. Just as I was about to dive into the job hunt again, my cell phone rang. My dad's name came across the screen. The last couple of years I had shuddered with guilt when I would see this, but now I was excited.

"Hi, Dad. How are you?" I answered, relieved to hear from him.

"Fine, son, how are you?" he asked, the same relief that I felt in his voice. "And how are your wife and that little angel?" *He's gone soft*, I thought to myself.

"They're fine. Seanna keeps asking about you, too. I think she's wishing away the days until you come again. I think you rank right up there next to Santa Claus." He laughed; I could tell this pleased him.

Our conversation went on with small talk for about five minutes. During this time, I could tell he wanted to ask me something but was unsure how to bring it up. Finally he said,

"Can I ask you a business question?" That was the dad I remembered-straight to the business.

"Sure," I said happily. I had missed those days of his bouncing ideas off me for a second opinion on whatever he was thinking. The excitement in his voice told me that he missed them too and had waited for some time to discuss these ideas with me.

I had had a lot of time to think during the last six months, so I had come up with some ideas of my own to help the next company that hired me run more efficiently and even grow into a national, perhaps global, company. I was going to give my presentation in the next interview I would have in this line of work, but so far I had not had the chance. I pitched them to my dad to see what he thought of them.

"Thank you for calling, Dad. Call me any time you need to," I said, hoping he would.

"You can count on it, son, now that you're answering my calls," he chuckled.

"Tell Mom, 'Hi' for me," I said, ending the call and not giving him the chance to tease me for my stupid past behavior.

Seanna was still sleeping when Jenny arrived home, so I let Jenny wake her up. Jenny had not been able to spend a lot of alone time with Seanna, so I went to the gym to work out, giving them some "girl time" together. It had been over two weeks since my last visit, and I was starting to feel flabby. Both girls expressed excitement for the opportunity for girl time.

I ran through my workout faster than normal so that I could get home for prayer time. When I got out of the car, I could hear Jenny's dance music blaring on the stereo. I knew the girls were dancing, so I kept hidden and watched them for a while. Jenny was wearing an old college jazz dance leotard. It was black with what looked like red paint splashed across the front of it. She looked gorgeous. Seanna was dressed in pink tights that looked to be a little too big for her small five-year-old body and a swimsuit with a princess on it. I wasn't sure which one because I had never paid much attention to princesses before. The pink tutu she had on fit her just fine.

They were dancing to some hyped-up fairy-tale song, probably one that matched the princess on Seanna's suit. It was almost comical how Jenny would flutter around the room as though she had practiced this dance for months. Seanna was doing her best to keep up. She kept one eye on Jenny, waiting for the next move. Every so often, though, they would bump into each other, and the room would erupt into giggles and hisses.

I was just barely able to see them as I poked my head around the corner of the refrigerator. Jenny must have expected me to stay at the gym for my usual three-hour workout. She was not even watching for me, to avoid embarrassment. I knew if they saw me it was all over, and I would ruin their fun. At that moment I realized that, for the first time, my home felt like there was nothing missing. It felt complete, a happy place where I would rather be more than any other place in the world. Then my heart sank as I thought about what was going to happen when Seanna had to go back to the orphanage at the end of the holidays. Pain and sadness filled my body. Was this really a good idea to bring this child into our home? I knew Jenny was going to take it hard when that time came. This was the happiest that I had seen her for years. She really did make a wonderful mother.

"Ahhhhh!" An ear-piercing scream broke my meditation and brought me back to reality. Jenny had caught me and screamed at the top of her lungs. My cover was blown. Seanna darted into the front room, and Jenny hit the deck behind the sofa. I was not finished with *my* fun, though. I ran and jumped over the sofa, landing next to Jenny, who kept screaming as if she had just seen a mouse. I started tickling her until the screams became laughs. After Jenny started shouting that she was going to "pee in her tights," I ran to find Seanna. She had slid back behind the Christmas tree in the corner.

"Fe, fi, fo, fum, I smell a little girl in a dance suit," I said, pretending to look for her. "There she is!" I shouted, pointing at her. She opened her mouth as wide as she could. I have the feeling that the scream that would have come out could have blown out my eardrums. I bent down to get her out from behind the tree to tickle her, and she started kicking at me.

"Let's get him, Seanna," Jenny yelled, still laughing and running into the room. She jumped on me at a full run and squashed me to the ground like a pancake. Seanna crawled out from behind the tree and jumped on Jenny, hissing her little laugh.

After we had all tickled each other to the point of tears, we laid on the floor, panting. I leaned over to Jenny, gave her a kiss, and said, "You still got it. You look hot." She turned bright red, jumped up, and left to go get dressed. Seanna trotted after her.

On Wednesday, Seanna and I stayed indoors because there was a massive snowstorm outside. I was glad that Jenny had arrived at work before it hit. Seanna and I were going to go to the store, but when I asked Seanna if she wanted to go, she just looked out of the window at the blizzard and shook her head, "No." I was fine with that decision; we needed a downtime day. I resumed my search for a job, checking the Internet and papers. Seanna played quietly with some of the many toys Jenny had brought home.

"Our home is starting to look like a toy store," I told Jenny that night. She agreed to stop bringing toys home when I told her that Christmas was coming, and she was making it really difficult for me to decide what to get Seanna by bringing home all these toys. I was running out of options, as she would already have all of the toys she wanted. It was not as if Seanna were going to ask for anything anyway, it was not in her nature. She was always satisfied with what she had.

The storm was still raging the next day. Seanna had a hard time letting Jenny get in the car.

"I think she's afraid I'll get into a wreck like she did," Jenny softly said to me. Seanna shook her head, "Yes." I was at a loss for what to do, but Jenny just kneeled down, gave Seanna a hug, and asked, "Can we pray before I go?" Seanna clapped as she jumped up and down.

"Okay, I'll say it," I said. Seanna then kneeled down on the kitchen floor. I looked at Jenny, and she motioned for me to do the same.

After I was finished praying for Jenny's safety, letting God know how important she was to Seanna and me, and saying that we really needed her to come home safely, Jenny stood up, crying, and gave me a hug.

"Thanks. I needed that," she said, sobbing. I must have done a good job because Seanna was satisfied enough to let her leave.

"Today we need to clean the house," I announced after Jenny pulled away. Seanna just gave me a "That's no fun" face.

"I know, but if you'll help me, then I'll let you choose what we do after we're done." Seanna smiled, clapped, and ran for the cleaning closet. They must have had the kids do the cleaning at the orphanage because this little girl could clean. I think she could clean better than I could. She proved it, too; she shook her head when I tried to use the wrong cleaner to scrub the toilets.

After we had cleaned the house from top to bottom, I asked, "Okay. Now what would you like to do?" Seanna decided that it was about time that I was up to speed on my princesses. She ran and got a stack of movies, and we had a movie marathon, stopping only for lunch and potty breaks.

"Tonight we'll have dinner alone. Jenny's going to be late because she has a doctor's appointment," I mentioned to Seanna as the last movie ended. I tried not to think of what might be wrong. Jenny was already struggling with her self-worth as a woman, not being able to have children. *I hope she won't have to endure another trauma on top of it.* Seanna must have realized I was worried, so she made up a new game for us to play as we were eating dinner. She was a master at coming up with fun, new games to keep my mind occupied.

Mac & Cheese had lost its touch, so I cooked the frozen pizza we had grabbed on our last shopping trip. I found out that it was the next best thing to my famous Mac & Cheese, from Seanna's point of view anyway. *We really need to go to the store again*, I thought. Then, I remembered that Santa was going to be at the grocery store on Friday and Saturday. *I could take Seanna to sit on Santa's lap, and perhaps I could overhear…Oh wait…that's a dumb idea.* What was she going to do? How could she tell Santa what she wanted for Christmas? I felt hopeless. I guess she would just have to live with what we decided to get her. She would, too. I was sure she would be fine with whatever we gave her, but I would really have liked to get her something she truly wanted. Maybe she could write it in a note. She seemed to be good at that. Maybe she would even ask Jenny or me to help her write it. I just had to prepare her for it.

"I saw a poster that said Santa was going to be at the store tomorrow," I mentioned unexpectedly, interrupting the game. She seemed surprised. "I'll take you so you can sit on his lap and…and give him a list of the presents you want for Christmas so that you can take them back to the orphanage with you," I said excitedly. Seanna stared at me in disappointment and disbelief. Not the reaction I was hoping for at all.

"What? I can help you write your list if you want," I said, trying to figure out what was wrong. Seanna jumped up, started crying, and gave me a "You don't get it" look. She ran to her room, slammed the door, and locked it.

"What? Seanna! What did I say?" I pleaded, following her.

She had been in there for an hour before Jenny's headlights came through the window. Nothing I could say would make her open her door to me. I could tell she was very upset by her sobbing. I felt horrible, and the worst part was that I did not know what I had done, so I could not fix it. I was very relieved when Jenny came through the door.

"She hates me," I said before Jenny could say anything.

"What?" she asked, surprised.

"I don't know what I said, but it made her very upset, and she won't let me in to talk to her about it," I said solemnly.

"What were you talking about?"

"We were talking about Santa."

"Santa?"

"Yeah, go figure. I told her I would help her write her Christmas list so that she could give it to him, and she got upset and locked herself in her room and has been there ever since."

"I'll go see if she'll talk to me." Jenny went over to Seanna's door and knocked.

"Seanna, can I come in?" There was a moment of silence, and then I heard footsteps, and the door unlocked. Jenny walked in, and the door closed and locked again.

You would think I was waiting for my child to be born. That was how nervous I was, waiting for Jenny to emerge from that room.

"She's really upset. What did you do?"

"I don't know. Maybe she hates Santa. Did you find anything out?"

"No, she was too upset to help me understand. She just cried herself to sleep. I'm sure she'll be over it in the morning," Jenny said confidently.

"She hates me."

"Max, I've watched Seanna with you these last couple of weeks, and I am confident that you are her most favorite person in the whole world," Jenny said. I know she said this to make me feel better, but it actually made me feel worse. I felt I had betrayed Seanna, and she could no longer trust me. I felt like I had lost my only child.

"What can I do?" I asked, hoping for some guidance.

"Don't worry about it tonight. She'll get over it. Children are very forgiving."

I was giving myself a headache worrying about it, so I changed the subject. "How was work? How was the doctor's appointment?" Jenny's countenance changed suddenly.

"He wants to see me again soon," she answered.

"Why? What's wrong?" I asked, all of my nightmares confirmed by her words.

"My family is coming Sunday," she said to change the subject again. In this situation, these were the best words she could have used. I instantly forgot about her illness.

"They are?" I asked, petrified. They lived so far away; they usually only visited the week after Christmas.

"They wanted to come and meet Seanna before Christmas."

"Yeah, I suppose they want to see how I'm doing as a father figure," I said disappointingly.

"Max, you know they don't judge you like that." Jenny tried to comfort me, but even she knew it was true. She looked grateful, though, that she had managed to bury the medical issue.

"Yeah, right," I mumbled, wanting to change the subject again. Her parents always thought she had married the wrong man. Two weeks before our wedding, they had refused to participate in the preparations. I had arrived at the house early to pick Jenny up for a concert that we were attending. Jenny had not yet arrived home from school, so I was cornered-literally cornered. It was the happiest, I think, I had ever seen them at having me at their house. It was the first time I had ever been there without Jenny. I tried to leave by telling them I would be back later, but they invited me in, with big smiles on their faces. They sat me in the corner of the dining room. I felt like a dunce and knew nothing good was going to come out of whatever they had to say. And I was right. They proceeded to cast their judgments about how worthless I was and that they hoped Jenny came to her senses before the wedding. Apparently, I did not have the right last name. I could never make enough money to support her, or them, as I found out later. I would never make a good husband, and there were a million other reasons.

When Jenny finally came home a half hour later, she noticed immediately after walking in the door that her parents had finally had their chance to chastise me. She just strolled calmly over to me and gave me a big kiss, apologizing for being late. As soon as she kissed me, I instantly forgot everything that her parents had said. I think they noticed it, too. They both looked disgusted that she would even think of kissing me in front of them. Then we left the house without her saying a word to them.

Jenny has always had that effect on me. She has always been able to get me to forget unpleasant things. Kissing her and staring into those deep brown eyes turns my brain into mush. If I were ever set on fire, I'd bet she could make me forget that I was burning.

I did not sleep much that night. I kept thinking of the dreaded visit from Jenny's parents. The only thing worse than them was her little, spoiled-rotten, 18-year-old sister. I always pictured their relationship like a Cinderella story, with Jenny being Cinderella. I felt like all my worries were engulfing my soul: no job, Jenny's family, Jenny's illness, and, of course,

Seanna. The situation with Seanna seemed to have drowned out the rest of my hardships. I had no clue what I had done, and it was killing me because without knowing what was wrong, there was no way for me to fix it. I ran through our conversation multiple times, but it was of no use. Obviously, I was no good at this parenting stuff.

Sleep must have found a way to knock me out because I had a dream. I was chasing a car down the street, and Seanna was in the back seat, looking at me and waving. The person driving the car looked like her, but was too old to be one of her parents. I remember not wanting her to go, so I started running and shouting after her, "Please don't go! She's mine! She's mine!" I awoke to a soft little hand touching my arm as it hung over the side of the bed. Despite the softness of it, it still startled me and I bolted upright in bed yelling, "Seanna, don't go. You're mine! I'm so sorry!" When I gathered my wits about me, I realized that I had failed to hear Seanna approaching our room. She had entered to wake me up. After looking at the clock, it dawned on me that she had waited for ten or so minutes before coming to wake me. I looked at Jenny, who was also startled. She gave me a "you jerk" look and rolled over. Then I noticed Seanna rolling on the floor. At first, I thought I might have hit her when I jumped, but then I noticed she was laughing. It was one of those good belly-busting laughs. I quickly climbed out of bed and took her to the kitchen. We were both laughing now.

Jenny was right. Whatever I had done the night before, she must have decided to forgive me. Seanna was her usual self and even reenacted my jumping out of bed when she startled me. I did not care though; she was happy with me again. We both laughed until we were crying. Jenny finally emerged from the bedroom to find us both red-faced, with splitting side-aches. It all started over again when we had to explain to Jenny the cause of our merriment. As she watched the ree-nactment of Seanna's sneaking up and startling me, she laughed so hard, and for so long, that she had a hard time staying on task and was almost late for work by the time she left.

The day went on as usual. I was glad for the child-like for-giveness that Seanna gave me. I spent most of my day pon-dering forgiveness. Was it really that easy to forgive others like a child can? Or, for a dad to forgive a son like mine had done? Or, for a loving spouse to forgive the other repeatedly, throughout a life together, as Jenny had forgiven me so many times?

That afternoon, I loaded Seanna into the car, not telling her where we were going. After all, I had no idea what had set her off, and I was not going to go through that again. I fig-ured I would ask forgiveness of her again if it was the whole Santa Claus thing. We arrived at the store just as they opened the ropes to let the kids, and their parents, line up to sit on Santa's lap. Even though we arrived when the sign said Santa would arrive, there were still a lot of people in front of us. Seanna did not seem to mind that this was the reason we had left the house. In fact, she looked just as excited as the rest of the children. After all, how could a person not be excited with all the children smiling and laughing while waiting for Santa?

The store had transformed its front entrance into a wonderful replica of Santa's workshop. Somebody had worked some long hours on the wooden background. The red and green decorations were hung with a flawless perfection. Santa sat on a chair in the corner of the half-wooden structure. The chair he was sitting on looked like a wooden throne that was painted gold and had a plump, red cushion. The elves, who looked to be teenager volunteers, were dressed in green and gold with elf-like hats. All of Santa's helpers were playing their parts wonderfully, which helped add to the excitement and magic of the scene.

Santa had the usual red suit with white fur trim on the cuffs, collars, and around the buttons. His beard was real, white, and full, bushier than most Santa beards. His rosy cheeks were not created by makeup either; they were real, too. His deep blue eyes were twinkling with happiness at the sight of all the animated children. His hat sat on his head slightly tilted to one side, and the bells on the end of his hat, and on the leather sash, rang out with every "Ho Ho Ho, Merry Christmas!" that Santa belted to the crowd.

"I hope they're paying this man extra because he is so good," I whispered to myself.

I was still unsure how this was going to go with Seanna. I had not dared to ask her if she wanted help writing a list to give to Santa. I had not noticed Jenny helping her either. As we got closer to the front of the line, I did notice that Seanna had pulled a note out of her pocket, and she looked more excited than ever to give it to him. I tried to see what was on the note, but she acted as if she were guarding it from me.

Finally, it was our turn. Seanna trotted up to Santa, and he helped her onto his lap. She looked like a little elf compared to the bigness of Santa. "Now aren't you a little cutie?" he said in a chuckling voice. Some of the elves came over to fuss over her, too.

"I know I don't even have to ask you if you've been good because something tells me you are as good as an angel," he laughed, his belly shaking with cheer. Seanna was beaming.

"So, with that question out of the way, what would you like for Christmas?" Santa asked. She handed him the note. Santa's twinkling eyes glanced at the little paper, and then at the scar under Seanna's chin. Slowly, it dawned on him that perhaps she could not speak. He gave me an understanding look, and then he read the message on the note. He seemed puzzled for a second and then told her, "I'll do my best on this one, and I think I have some other ideas as well. You have a Merry Christmas."

I was perplexed by Santa's solemn tone. What did the note say? I walked up to help Seanna off Santa's lap and to get her treat from one of the elves.

"I think you can help her with this one more than Santa can," Santa said tenderly, slipping me the note. Seanna was busy with one of the elves, so I snuck a peek before slipping it into my pocket.

On the little note was written "New Family." Suddenly, the drama of the previous night made perfect sense. This child once had what Jenny and I had yearned for so badly, a family to call our own. Then she had lost hers. Her yearning must have been even greater than ours because she once knew what it was like to be a part of a family. The night before, when I had asked her what she wanted to get to take back to the orphanage, I must have broken her heart. She did not want to go back. She wanted a family. She only wanted what all humanity, deep down, needs: a loving, caring family to call their own. She wanted a family to love her, care for her, cry with her, and laugh with her. We had been doing this for the last couple of weeks. Was it a possibility that we could do it for the rest of our lives? I had never even thought about it. I pondered over this question as we walked to the car. *How does a person even begin to adopt a child?*

Seanna was very quiet on the ride home. She was just taking in the sights of Christmas as I drove through town, which was good because my mind was racing. Could we do this? Could I be Seanna's dad? My heart fluttered. *I would love that. I want that. But, does she want me?* I obviously had a lot to learn; I did break her heart the previous night, after all. I knew Jenny would say yes. She loved Seanna as much as I did. Could Seanna still have family searching for her? It had only been one year; suppose they found her. Yet, the orphanage staff and the sheriff said they had called off the search and that there was no trace of a family. Could somebody have already started the adoption process on her? Suddenly, the dream from last night came to mind. My heart broke. *I cannot let that happen. I know that I love this little girl and want her to be mine.* Seanna's warm hand touched my cheek. I was crying. "I'm okay," I lied. I could not let her be somebody else's daughter.

I made up my mind just seconds before pulling in the drive and seeing Jenny's car. I was going to the orphanage tomorrow to find out the answers to my questions. I thought it best to keep this to myself; Jenny did not need another disappointment and more heartache if the adoption did not work out.

Chapter 8

"Saturday," I said to myself as I got out of bed. Seanna had decided to sleep in, so it was the passing cars outside that had woken me. The three of us had stayed up late the night before watching a movie. It was one that Seanna had made me watch during our movie marathon, but I still didn't know which princess it was in the story. The effect was different, though, with Jenny sitting there. The two of them cried during the sad parts, oohed and awed over the princess' pretty dress, and cried again at the end. I got an elbow to the ribs when I started laughing at the both of them during the first tears they shed. I was having a hard time paying attention because I kept thinking of what I was going to do the next day. *I must have really been in a trance*, I thought, rubbing my bruised ribs from all the elbows I had received by not giving Jenny the comforting hugs she needed during the movie. It brought a smile to my face when I thought of all the times I had had sore ribs when we were dating; Jenny had loved dragging me to all the sappy romance movies playing in town.

First up on my list today, I thought as I got out of bed, *is going straight to the orphanage to find out about adopting Seanna and then taking the first steps to get the process started.*

Despite my anxiety and excitement the previous night, I had been able to keep all of it a secret from Jenny. I did mention, however, that I had to go into town in the morning. Jenny had asked why, but Seanna interrupted us during the conversation, so that was as far as it went. Thank goodness. I was a terrible liar, and Jenny usually saw straight through me. I was glad for the reprieve.

Never had I been so jittery about a day before. I was like a little boy on Christmas Eve, thinking of the new bike that Santa was bringing. I was finished with breakfast before Jenny came into the kitchen, Seanna trotting in right behind her.

"I didn't hear you get up, Seanna," I said, surprised. "Seanna spent half the night in our room, dear," Jenny said, smiling. "She had a nightmare about the mean man in the princess movie last night," she finished. Seanna blushed shyly. *That was odd*, I thought. After all this child had been through, she had a nightmare about some cartoon man wearing tights. I guess when I was a kid I used to have nightmares about the bad man on the Smurfs. I thought it was probably best if I kept that to myself though.

"She came into our room at about one a.m. last night. I caught her just as she was about to touch you again. Good thing, too; I didn't want a repeat of yesterday morning," Jenny said with a smirk. Seanna hissed, her whole body bouncing.

"I can't believe I didn't hear you. But you know what, Seanna?" I asked. She shook her head, "No."

"You don't have anything to worry about. You know why?" Again, she shook her head no. I held up my arm and pointed to my bicep.

"I've got these big guns that are guaranteed to scare away all bad people, and monsters, and any other thing that goes bump in the night." Seanna's eyes widened as if to believe every word. Jenny snickered, trying to hold back a good laugh.

"That is, if he can wake up before the bad things haul him off," Jenny snorted, laughing.

"You're ruining the moment," I said jokingly. Seanna came over to examine my arm more closely. Jenny could not stop her laugh this time, and neither could I. Once again, laughter filled our home. There was no other way to describe what Seanna brought into our lives, other than pure joy. Was this what our home was going to be like if Seanna stayed? More moments like this, a home filled with laughter, with this child at its center? Now, if I could only pull off the adoption.

Suddenly, there was a knock at the door; the moment was over. I looked at the clock. It was just about eight. Who could that be? I got up and went to the door, the girls following me. I opened it.

"He *is* out of bed," they both said as if they had made a bet about it.

"Mom, Dad! Rachel!" Jenny said, brushing past me as I stood at the door with my mouth wide open, speechless.

"You're here early," Jenny said, surprised.

"We wanted to surprise you." *No surprise they came early*, I thought to myself. *They were probably trying to catch me in bed, on purpose, confirming their thoughts of me as a mongrel.* They were always trying to prove to Jenny that she had made a mistake by choosing me over that little, spoiled, rich boy she had been dating before me. Even when I had a job and things were going well, they continued to discredit me. Jenny just kept telling me to ignore it, but I could tell it bothered her as much as it did me.

"Welcome to our home," I said, trying to announce my authority over my dominion. It was of no use, though. They had slipped past me and were already critically inspecting Seanna. I just stood in the doorway, trying to look as though I were a general, ready to give a command.

"Close the door, boy. Are you trying to give me pneumonia?" Jenny's mom blurted out. Then I, the general, fell off my horse and obeyed.

Jenny's sister had already started barking out orders at her. "Take my coat. I need a drink. Not water; chocolate milk will do. Bring me a chair." Jenny obeyed her every command. I guessed it was because she wanted them to feel welcomed. It was odd to see how Rachel got so jealous of Seanna and the attention she was getting.

After an hour of constant criticism mixed with demands and trying to be polite, I was done. How many times and in how many ways could they mention that I was un-employed? How many requests could three people make? If they had their way, then they would march Jenny straight down to the attorney's office and start the divorce papers today. They offered several times to let her come live back at home if we lost the house. That offer, of course, did not include me, just her, and they let us know that. It never bothered me though; I would rather be dropped in a frozen river than to live with them. My only fear was that Jenny might take them up on the offer. So far, she had put up with both them and me. A couple of months ago I was afraid that she was ready to leave me, but she hung in there for who knows what reason, and now there was no way she was going to leave. Our relationship had never been better since Seanna came to us. We were strong together now; so, this time her family was going to know it.

"Jenny, you look dead on your feet. You look ill," Jenny's mom said, seeing her hold her stomach.

"No, I just haven't had breakfast yet," she admitted. Her mom ignored her.

"Overworked, you are," her mom said, looking at me angrily. I bit my tongue. I would bet the three of us looked overworked since they would not let us relax.

"I'll bet taking care of this child by yourself and working at the hospital has been hard on you," Jenny's father said, coming to her aid and helping her get up out of the chair as if she were an invalid. That was it! I was losing it! There was no way

I was going to listen to this for two days. It was bad enough when I thought it was just going to be Sunday, but now it was an extra day. No way! I had to set them straight. I shot out of my chair. Jenny stepped in front of my face and kissed me, as if to tell her parents, "This is my husband, and I love him." She must have sensed that I was about to lose it. After all, I was the one taking care of Seanna and doing a good job of it, too. I thought I heard Jenny's mom gasp with disgust. Seanna must have sensed the tension. She took Jenny's parents by the hands and led them from the room. The brat-of-a-sister followed, trying to get in between Seanna and Jenny's mom.

"Don't you have to go into town today, honey?" Jenny asked as I glared at them leaving the room.

"Yes I do," I blurted angrily.

"Maybe now is a good time," she suggested, pleading with her eyes.

"Yes, now is the perfect time," I said, gritting my teeth.

I got in the car and drove into the city. I was so infuriated that I almost forgot where I was going. Anywhere but home was good enough for me. As I pondered that thought, sadness came into my heart. I had let anger come back into my life. It was a feeling that did not belong, especially around Seanna and Jenny. It was a feeling I had not felt for a couple of weeks now. My home had been such a safe, inviting place lately. I used to dread being home on some days, before Seanna arrived, but I think that was because I had forgotten what a true home was supposed to be. Lately, our home had felt like a home should: a safe harbor, a place of refuge, joy and comfort. I hoped all would go back to normal once this weekend ended and Jenny's family was gone. Then I had a frightening thought. If adoption were not a possibility, then would our home return to the rocky harbor it had once been, one of no laughter and with happy moments few and far between the disappointments? I loved Jenny and could not bear to lose her, but could we keep our home so inviting if we had to do it alone, with no Seanna?

I was driving around aimlessly for a while, trying to calm down before heading to the orphanage. The drive was not helping, so I decided to go to a toy store and look for possible presents for Seanna. As I was walking around the store, I could not help but feel out of place. There were so many things to choose from, but I had no idea what to buy.

I was in the doll section when I heard a woman say, "Mr. Fox?" I spun around and realized that she was the woman from church who had a daughter the same age as Seanna.

"Oh, hi," I said politely.

"I thought that was you. How are you?" she inquired.

"Fine, thank you, and yourself?" I said, trying to sound convincing.

"Good! How are your wife and Seanna?"

"They're doing well." I was not really in the mood for small talk, but she persisted.

"Are you here shopping for Seanna for Christmas?"

"Yes, and I have no idea what to get her," I admitted. I think the woman could tell I was frustrated, so she offered some suggestions.

"Julia is Seanna's age, and she's really wanted this toy over here," she suggested.

By the time I left the store, with the help of Mrs. Casper I had all of my Christmas shopping done for Seanna. I felt great. Mrs. Casper said to call her if I had any more questions about little girls, but that seemed a little weird to me. The last thing she asked me was if we were going to church the next day. I told her we were planning on it. Seanna had quizzed both Jenny and me about it the previous night before bed. She made us cross our hearts, so that meant no backing out of it. Besides, I knew Jenny's parents were not church-going people, so it would be a much needed break.

After my shopping success, I was ready to research the adoption. I finally pulled into the orphanage parking lot, parked the car, and ran inside. Miss Hinder was sitting at her desk, looking almost exactly as she had the night I first met Seanna.

"Well, hello, Mr. Fox. How are you today?" she asked, shocked to see me.

"I'm okay," I said nervously. "I have a question," I said, getting right to the point.

"Sharon just got back from your place, and she said you weren't there." I looked shocked. I forgot about that weekly meeting, and we were both supposed to be there.

"Oh, I'm sorry. I forgot," I said sheepishly.

"That's quite all right. Your wife filled her in on why you had to go to town today. Sharon said you had some very interesting visitors for the weekend."

"What did they say?" I asked, getting ready to defend myself. They better not have messed this up for me. If, for some reason, we were not able to adopt Seanna because of something they had said about me, it would be the end of my relationship with them. Miss Hinder must have read my expression.

"Oh, she didn't say much, but she did mention that she herself was very glad to get out of there," she said, laughing. I relaxed a little. Those vampires must also have badgered poor Sharon. I felt sorry for her.

"Your question was?" Miss Hinder reminded me, smiling.

"Oh, I was wondering how hard it would be, and what we would have to do, in order to adopt Seanna."

"Well, Mr. Fox, this is a little out of character for you, isn't it?" she joked.

"I know it's only been a short while, but I really have been doing well with her, and we love her so much," I said, defending my question.

"Relax, Max," she chuckled at the rhyme. "You don't have to defend your position to me. Actually, I knew from the first time we met that this was going to happen eventually. With you, I thought it would take a little longer. That Seanna does have some sort of magic, doesn't she?"

"Yes, she does," I admitted. "So, is adoption hard, and how much time does it take?"

"Well, Mr. Fox, I'm sorry to tell you this, but Seanna is unable to be adopted at this time," she said somberly. My heart broke. I felt like the air had just been sucked out of the room. I was slowly dying.

"Why not?" I gasped.

"This state has a law that says that a missing person with no family, like Seanna, has to be in the state's custody for two years while they try to find a family member. So, Seanna is not eligible for one more year." I was heartbroken, and I knew Jenny and Seanna would be, too. Would Seanna understand why we had to send her back? It was just not fair. My mind went to the note I still had at home: "New Family." My eyes were misty, and I suddenly realized how bad I wanted this to happen.

"So, there's nothing I can do?"

"I'm so sorry. Not at this time," Miss Hinder said compassionately, I think even she felt my heart break

"However," she continued. I looked up hopefully at the change in her voice. "You can be her foster parents until that time, and if there has not been a change in her case at that point, then you may adopt her," she said joyfully. I just sat there, staring, with my mouth open. She had totally led me on. What a mean thing to do. I was about to retaliate when it hit me; we could have Seanna stay at our home. I jumped up and gave Miss Hinder a hug, shouting praises the whole time.

"So, what do we have to do to be able to do this?" I crowed.

"Well, after Sharon's first visit, she gave me the report of how you two wanted to know as much about Seanna as possible. In my experience, that means the couple is thinking of adopting the child. So, I've already taken care of it; you are good to go, Mr. Fox," she said, smiling. I was stunned; I was unable to move for what seemed like minutes, but was probably only seconds.

"Thank you, you have no idea how much this means to us!" I screamed as I jumped out of my chair.

"Oh, I think I do," she said, putting her finger in her ear as if I had destroyed her ear drums.

I returned home that evening just in time for dinner. I figured I could handle Jenny's parents, no matter how bad they were, after the news Miss Hinder had given me. When I came through the door smiling, I think Jenny's parents took offence to it. It probably confused them that I was so happy to be in the same room as them.

During dinner, I did not pay attention to the conversation between Jenny and her parents. I found it best to ignore it. Seanna caught on too, and I could tell she was not impressed with Jenny's parents or sister at all. I tried to keep her occupied so that she did not have to hear the negative criticism coming from the other side of the table. Jenny's parents seemed to be frustrated that I was not paying attention to them, or their remarks, because they kept getting louder and louder. I did notice a couple of remarks aimed at me, each one worse than the one before. Finally, after we cleaned up the remains of dinner, we migrated to the living room.

Jenny's mom blurted out, "These couches are so uncomfortable!"

"Now, dear," Jenny's dad said as if he were going to defend us. "I'm sure they would have bought better ones if Max had any skills to get a good job." I heard that one.

"Yeah, like, I'm surprised that they let Seanna come to your house. Obviously, by the way she acts, you aren't helping her," Rachel added. That was it! My whole body instantly started to twitch with rage. I was just about to lose my control after that comment when Jenny exploded instead.

"Get out of my house!" she shouted, breaking the silence.

"Oh, Jenny dear, don't overreact," her mom said, realizing that they had stepped over the line.

"Get out, all of you. I have sat here all day listening to you and your criticism, taking your orders, and I do not welcome it here. You have put down the man I love, who is doing his best to take care of Seanna and me. He has been trying to find a job almost every day. He's been the best father figure that I could ever imagine for Seanna, and he loves me despite the family I come from." Even though it was out of character, I actually enjoyed her outburst and hoped it would not stop.

"Don't have a cow, Sis," Rachel said, somehow not seeing the danger she was in.

"You spoiled little brat! You have no idea what life is all about. This is my home, which felt just like what a home should be—warm, loving and inviting—until you all showed up. Sis, if you don't grow up and take your head out of the clouds, then you'll never know what it feels like to have a home like this. I didn't know until I left the house you're in and married Max. You'll never know true love, or how your heart could be whole, unless you have a man who loves you the way Max loves me. Some people search a lifetime to find what we have and never find it because they were unwilling to give what it takes. You will never know how wonderful it is to be called "Mother" from a child who truly loves you. These things don't happen to people who can't see past their own selfishness and think only of receiving." Jenny said, almost pleading, trying to turn this into a teaching moment for her sister.

"You don't have to defend him, Jenny," her dad said, grasping for straws. That was the absolute worst thing to say. If Jenny was mad before, it did not even compare to what she was now. Her whole body was shaking, but her voice did not even quiver. She sounded steady and strong.

"I want you all to leave. I don't want you in my home again until you realize how you should treat us," came the words in a calm, firm tone. Seanna went over to the door and opened it. They stared at each other for a second, and then looked at me. I smiled. "Get out!" Jenny shouted as her mom opened her mouth to speak. Seanna appeared with their coats. They stood up and left without another word. Seanna slammed the door behind them, turned around, leaned against the door, and blew some hair out of her face. Seanna looked as though she were saying, "It's exhausting to deal with such people!" I looked at Jenny worriedly, wondering what she might do next.

"That felt great!" she shouted, relieving her tension. Seanna clapped. I gave Jenny a big hug and a kiss, thanking her for finally standing up to her parents. It just would not have been the same if I had done it, as I had done so many times before. Obviously, it never did any good.

Just like that, we got our happy place back and were able to enjoy the rest of the evening together. Seanna and I did try to step a little lighter around Jenny, just in case there was some of that contention still lingering. I had never seen her act that way before, but I guess even the gentlest cats will defend their territory if threatened.

Jenny appeared to be mostly over the confrontation with her parents by the time we were all ready for church the next morning. I was a little worried that she might start feeling bad about it. I did not have to worry long, though, because whenever she would think about it, she would come and find me, looking for a hug, and then she would whisper in my ear, "They deserved it." She said it as though comforting me, but I knew it was more for her justification of the situation. It did not matter to me how she dealt with it. I was just glad it had happened. I was determined to be there to support her. I thought I had loved her before, but hearing her stand up to her family like that had tightened the unbreakable cords around our hearts.

Seanna was excited to be going to church again, and actually, we were too. I told Jenny about the help I had received at the toy store from Mrs. Casper, and she wanted to thank her personally for helping me. So far, that was the only reason I had given her for going into town the day before, and I wanted to keep it that way for as long as I could. This was going to be my Christmas surprise to her and to Seanna.

Once inside the church, I realized that everybody was making it a point to say "Hi" and to introduce themselves to us. It almost seemed like they had been primed to do so. Even if they were primed, it was still okay. It made us feel welcome. Just before the third class, Jenny finally caught up with Mrs. Casper.

"Thank you so much for helping my husband yesterday at the store. You have no idea how much he needed it," Jenny said gratefully.

Mrs. Casper replied back, just loud enough so I could hear, "He had this lost puppy dog look on his face, so I just had to rescue him." They both giggled, then disappeared into the class.

The focus at church that day was on Jesus Christ. As we were getting ready for bed that evening, Jenny and I discussed what we had learned in our groups. We both marveled at the life of Christ.

Here was this man, the son of God, who taught the world about love, kindness, and charity through his teachings and his life. In that moment, the reasoning behind Seanna's notes suddenly began to be clear to me. *She truly is a remarkable and special little girl.* Here was this little girl who had gone through so much adversity in her short life, yet she was spreading Christ's loving message through her one-word notes.

"It kind of brings purpose to your life when you think about it that way, like He knows exactly who you are," Jenny said loudly, noticing that my mind had strayed from the conversation. Obviously, she was not finished with her thought.

"How could He not know who we are after going through all that pain for us?" They were the last words of our conversation that night, and then we both fell asleep.

The first part of the next week went by faster than ever.

"I can't believe it's Friday again," I mentioned to Jenny before she left for work.

"I know. Remember when you were a kid and you would wish away the time so Christmas would come sooner?" Jenny asked.

"Yeah, then once it was there you couldn't slow it down, and it was all over again," I said, reminiscing about my childhood. I could tell by the solemn tone in her voice that Jenny was trying not to think of the short time we had left with Seanna. The thought of it was really hurting her. I was determined to keep the foster parenting and adoption a secret, so I just gave her a hug.

"It seemed like as soon as school got out for the break, time went twice as fast," she added with a sigh, trying to take her mind off her painful thoughts.

"Oh! The kids get out of school today, don't they?" I asked her, my voice sounding panicked.

"Yes," she answered.

"I still haven't taken Seanna to see Robert Doss at his school."

"What?" Jenny looked at me for some understanding.

"I promised Seanna that I would take her to see Robert Doss, the boy who saved her. The sheriff said the best place to catch him would be after school."

"Most of the mothers at work are getting off before noon today to pick up their kids from school because of the holiday break, so you'd better go before that," she said, kissing me good-bye. I still was not sure it was a good idea, but I had promised Seanna that I would take her.

I decided to make it a surprise and not tell Seanna where we were going. I was getting pretty good at keeping secrets these days. The fact that she did not ask me anymore where we were going whenever we got in the car also helped. I did not know what was going to happen when we got there, or if we would even find Robert. I did have a desire to talk to him if he wanted to see us. I wondered if a young man who was left as maimed as he was for the rest of his life would ever regret the decision he had made to help Seanna escape.

I pulled into the school parking lot just as the students were exiting the building and found a parking spot near the front door. I got out and went to get the door for Seanna. I opened the door, and as I was undoing her seat belt, I heard some commotion coming from the school steps. At the school entrance, a group of kids was throwing snowballs at everyone who was leaving. The excitement of getting out for the break must have instigated the activity. Then, I heard one of the young men shout as he hit an innocent bystander.

"Hey, Scar Face! Does Santa Claus come to the homes of the ugly, or do you scare all the reindeer away?" Another snowball from a different boy hit the boy in the head. He turned to face his attackers, obviously very angry. Even from where I was standing, about sixty feet away, I could tell that the facial features of this young man were not right and were badly distorted. His scars traveled up his head, under his hat, and down to his shirt. You could tell that his face was not the only part of his body that was scarred. The sheriff was right. I instantly knew that this must be Robert. There was only one thing that could cause scars to look like his: fire. The young men taunted the disfigured boy as he approached them. Robert was much bigger than they were, but they outnumbered him. I could tell this meeting was not going to end well. More students were now gathering around, while others pretended not to notice. One or two also ran back into the school, possibly to look for a teacher. I could tell they were not going to make it back out in time, so I told Seanna, "Stay in the car, and I'll be right back." As I said this, I noticed that she was no longer in the car. She had slipped by me without my even knowing. I saw her disappear between two cars as she ran towards the group of kids.

"Seanna!" I called out, but she could not hear me over the boys' shouting.

"No!" I shouted again. I knew that if a fight broke out, the last thing they would watch out for would be a child. They would trample her before even realizing she was there. I started to run for her, but she had already reached the group of students near the school steps.

I ran harder, but then I heard one of the kids yell, "Hold it, stop!"

Then another added, "Where did she come from?" I reached the gathering and pushed my way through to the center. Seanna was pushing the young man that had started the taunting. He was standing face to face with the scarred young man. The mean boy scooted back a couple of steps while the scarred boy held his ground.

"What the...." shouted the troublemaker. Seanna then turned around, ran to the disfigured young man, and hugged his legs.

"Are you Robert?" I asked feeling out of place.

"Who's this? Your little girlfriend?" the boy teased Robert, unaware of my presence.

"No," I said, looking straight at the instigator. The rest of the students froze, realizing that a grown-up had busted them.

Seanna pulled out a note and gave it to Robert: "Savior." I was barely able to read the note from my position in the group. Seanna was sobbing on Robert's shoulder now. He had bent down to hug her when he realized who she was. I could tell the crowd was confused at what was taking place, so I filled them in.

"This is the little girl who Robert saved from the exploding car that left him with those scars," I said sternly. As everybody looked at his scars, including me, I could see that even though he had undergone plastic surgery, he would never be the same. Robert was sobbing now, holding on to Seanna as if he had just saved her from the crash.

"So, that's what happened to you, Rob?" broke the voice of the boy who had squared off to fight Robert, and he hung his head and stared at the ground. The others in the circle did the same.

"I'm sorry. I didn't know," another one said, unable to make eye contact. The rest of the boys followed with apologies. I wasn't sure how long we were there, but finally a man who I assumed was the principal came into the middle of the circle. He looked at me and then Seanna and seemed to understand the situation.

"All right, break it up, everybody. Go home and have a nice Christmas break." He then took the five young men back inside the school.

Robert spoke for the first time. "Seanna, I've wanted to see you for so long. There's not a burn on you. They told me so, but it was too hard to believe. I was so worried that you had to go through what I did, but you look just fine. They told me your throat, and voice, are damaged." He looked down to her scar. Seanna looked up at his face, touching his scarred cheek as if to say, "I'm sorry you were hurt for me." She started sobbing uncontrollably, burying her face in his neck.

"I'm okay," Robert said, trying to comfort her. I could tell by his words that he was a very tenacious person. He would have to be. Obviously, people had been hounding him for his looks without even knowing the situation.

Robert looked at me and said, wiping a tear from his eye, "I'm sorry, sir. I'm Robert Doss."

"I know who you are, and I thank you for being such a brave boy. We would be honored if you would let us drive you home."

Robert looked at the bus, his other alternative, and then said, "That would be great." I imagined that he was trying to avoid the awkward situation of the long ride home with the other students who had just witnessed the confrontation.

The ride to Robert's house was short; he only lived a couple of miles from the school. He sat in the back of the car with Seanna. She was so excited. Robert held her hand as we drove, but he did not say much. He asked Seanna some yes or no questions, so all she had to do was nod, or shake, her head. I asked Robert questions about his life and his family. I wondered how he had become so brave and steadfast. By the few questions I asked, I knew that he was no ordinary young man. The hero's mask that he wore could never do justice to the spirit he had within his heart. I frowned as this thought sank in. *People will probably never take him for the man he is because of his looks.*

Robert lived out past the suburbs, in the farming area that surrounded the city. The homes were separated by acres here, not feet, as they were in the city. His house was an older, rather large farmhouse that was built to look like a big red barn. Fields with roaming animals surrounded the house. It was breathtaking to see the snow-covered farm.

After we pulled into his long driveway, Seanna wanted to walk with Robert to his door. I went with them. At the door, Robert made Seanna promise to come and visit him again. After they both gave each other a hug, they said good-bye. Seanna touched his face again as if to say, "I'm sorry for this and for your pain."

"Now, don't you worry about these scars. It's not the scars that make the man; it's the man that make the scars. I earned these scars, and you are proof of that, so I don't mind them at all. Most people die wondering if they have done anything good with their life. I know, with a surety, that I have, and these scars help me remember that every day."

Seanna nodded her head, understanding what he meant. As we were turning to leave, a cat came around the corner of the house to greet us, followed by four kittens. Seanna lit up like a Christmas tree; she bent down to cuddle the kittens. I could see that we were not going to be leaving for a while, so I asked the question I had been burning to ask but did not want Seanna to hear the answer to. This moment just happened to be perfect because Seanna was preoccupied by chasing the kittens.

"Do you mind my asking you a question about the accident?" I asked carefully.

"No, sir," Robert answered.

"What happened the night of the crash?"

Robert took a deep breath, and then he began to tell me his story. "I was on my way home from the job I had just started. There was a terrible snowstorm that night. The wind was blowing, and there was a snowdrift on the road. I was following a semi-truck, which had a tanker of fuel. I could barely make out the lights of the oncoming car when the semi hit the snowdrift and careened into the opposite lane. The driver was helpless; it all happened so fast. He hit the car head-on. I also hit the drift and spun off the road in the opposite direction. The semi rolled over and spilled fuel everywhere, including on Seanna's car. I jumped out of my truck as fast as I could to try to help whomever I could. The truck driver was crawling out his passenger side door, looking dazed. I could tell he was okay though. I could see he had his cell phone in his hand, so I told him to call 911. It was then that I went around to the front of the truck. The car was on fire. I could tell the two people in the front seat were dead, but I could see Seanna's head moving slightly in the back seat. Without thinking, I ran to get her out of the car, but. when I got there, the door was crushed, but I managed to get it open. That's when I noticed the baby's car seat next to Seanna's seat. The baby was unresponsive, but I went for him first. It took me a second to figure out the car seat straps, but I got him free." His voice broke, and then he started to cry. "I carried him a safe distance away, took off my coat, and wrapped him in it to protect him from the snow…" He took a second to finish his sentence. "I had no idea he was already gone. They said he probably died on impact." Robert's face had a puzzled look on it as if he were reflecting back to see if he could have done anything more to save the baby. He shook his head and continued, "Running back, I saw that the fire had spread over most of the car. I knew that if I went back, then I would be burned. I hesitated for just one second, and then I don't know what happened. The only way I can describe it is that it must be what a soldier goes through during a battle. Whether it was duty, or just the sense of responsibility, I don't know, but there was no fear, and I didn't care what happened to me. Even though I didn't know the girl in that car, I felt as though it would have been the greatest honor a man could have if I died saving her. I just didn't want that little girl to get hurt." He glanced at the little angel trying to snuggle four kittens at once. "I was able to get Seanna out fast, but I was on fire," he continued, his face bunched up with the thought of the horrible pain. "And then the explosion…..I covered Seanna the best I could with my body….I don't remember much after that…" He trailed off.

"God bless you, Robert. God bless you," I choked out, fighting back tears.

"Oh He has, He has. With how badly I was burned, I should have in no way been alive today, but I am, thanks to Him. I just got out of the hospital four months ago. I'm grateful to be alive. It's been a rough year, but I would do it all again if I had to." I just stared at him for a minute or so as he bent down to help Seanna with the kittens. Seanna's note to him had said it all: "Savior." He truly was her savior. I realized that this young man was the first person I had ever met who was a true example of the Savior Jesus Christ.

I asked Robert some more questions about the investigation after the accident. He thought it was odd that nobody had mentioned that Seanna had a brother, but he admitted that the investigators had never asked him much about the baby either. I gave him my number and told him that he was always welcome to come over to our home at any time. We said our good-byes again and headed home.

Chapter 9

We had Robert come over the day before Christmas Eve. Jenny was dying to meet him, and I wanted to get to know him a bit better. I was amazed at the instant relationship that he and Seanna had formed. They acted as if they were brother and sister. I could tell that Robert wanted nothing more than to protect and help Seanna with her disability. He had even started learning sign language, which he was trying to teach Seanna. She was picking it up fast, so Jenny and I also wanted to learn. Since it was almost Christmas, Robert was teaching us the signs for words that had to do with the holiday.

"I have an aunt who knows sign language, and she said she would love to teach us," he said, half-asking, half-hoping. Seanna exploded, running around the room clapping and dancing.

"I'll take that as a 'yes' then." She grabbed him by the legs and hugged him. My parents arrived later that evening, just in time to meet Robert before he left.

"What a fine, outstanding young man," my father said as we all waved good-bye to Robert while he drove away. Then Dad turned around and scooped Seanna up into his arms. She was so excited to see my parents. They had brought a couple more presents, for Seanna of course, to add to the ones that she had not opened on their previous visit. They also had a few for Jenny and me. After we had added all of their presents to those that we had bought for them, the tree looked like a present factory that had gone haywire.

"Don't worry. They're just small things," my mom kept saying when I would comment on the number of gifts they had brought. I knew better though. They had been waiting for a grandchild to spoil for years.

I was a little disappointed when my mom told me that she had forgotten to bring her old nativity that I had asked her to bring.

"It's okay. I've just been thinking a lot about that and about all the stories you used to teach me about the true meaning of Christmas," I said disappointedly.

"I had it next to the door so I wouldn't forget it, but your dad was in such a hurry. I can't remember the last time I've seen your dad so happy. He's talked about nothing but Seanna, you, Jenny, and Christmas since our last visit," she laughed.

Jenny's parents called that night to apologize but stated that they did not know what they were apologizing for. After Jenny hung up the phone, I said, "You've got to give them some credit for trying."

"You give them credit if you want to. I will when they grow up," she threatened.

On Christmas Eve morning, we woke up to about a foot of snow on the ground.

"Looks like we'll have to entertain ourselves here this morning," I said sadly. We had planned on going to the mall and the city park to see all of the decorations and people. However, since it was a holiday, it would be later in the day before the city workers cleared the streets.

The morning ended up being not so bad after all. Dad and I were able to catch some of the games that were on TV. Seanna would interrupt us every once in a while to have us play with her. It was really not interrupting though; we were glad to do it. I got a kick out of watching my dad change the clothes on some of the dolls Seanna had given him. I could not stop laughing when I caught my dad in Seanna's closet, playing house. His big frame looked out of place sitting there, Indian-style, pretending to do the dishes. I had never seen this side of him before. He was usually all business and sports.

"I guess that's what a little girl does to you," he said, laughing, when I caught them. Jenny and my mom captured every moment they could by snapping pictures.

"That's a keeper," my mom would say after snapping one that she particularly liked. They all acted as if they wanted to catch every moment of the day to have it to remember for years to come. At times, I would see sadness on their faces as they thought of taking Seanna back to the orphanage. I overheard Jenny and my mom talking about it in the kitchen a couple of times. They spent a lot of time in the kitchen, probably so nobody would see them crying. They still had no idea about my gift that I was going to give all of them the next day.

It was about eleven o'clock in the morning when somebody knocked on the door.

"Robert!" I shouted, ushering him in. "How did you make it here?" I asked, thinking of the snowy roads. Everyone greeted him with a warm welcome. Seanna ran up and jumped into his arms. I could tell by the smile on his face that it made him feel happy.

"Did you walk here?" I asked. He was dressed unusually warm for a car ride. I could see that the scars on his neck had turned a deep purple from the cold.

"No. Our farm is only a couple of miles from here. I was wondering if I could take you all for a ride," he said anxiously.

As we looked out of the window, we all caught a glimpse of a team of horses and a big, beautiful, red sleigh. Seanna jumped up and down excitedly. None of us had ever ridden on a horse-drawn sleigh before.

"We would love to!" Jenny exclaimed, almost as excited as Seanna. We all ran to bundle up for the ride.

Once outside, we could fully appreciate the sight of the old-fashioned sleigh juxtaposed against the modern houses in the background. The horses, which were hitched to the front, were Clydesdales and were very big and beautiful. Their hair looked silky smooth, right down to the hooves. They were black with white spots and were majestic against the blanket of snow that covered everything in sight. They had a series of black leather straps, covered in jingle bells, which were hanging from the yokes and harnesses that tied them to the sleigh.

The sleigh itself was huge and painted a bright, shiny red. It was so shiny that it looked as though somebody had even waxed it. To me, it was the closest thing I had ever seen to what Santa's sleigh should look like. The front edge curled up to protect the driver from any kick-up from the horses. The driver was separated from the back compartment where the passengers rode. There were benches on both sides of the sleigh, which were made of a black material and arranged so that the passengers faced each other. The driver's seat had the same fabric on it. It was an awesome sight to behold..

"Santa," Seanna signed. Robert had taught her that sign the day before, and she had been very busy practicing it!

"Very good, Seanna, but no, it's not Santa's sleigh. I think my horses are too heavy to fly," Robert said, laughing.

The sleigh was so tall that we had to use the metal steps to climb into it. I supposed it had to be that way to accommodate the large horses that were pulling it.

Robert took us around the neighborhood at first, but when he could tell we were all comfortable, he ventured out further from home.

It was breathtaking-so much so that you could not feel the cold. We all just snuggled under blankets in the back of the sleigh. We laughed and pointed to things as we passed. The snow had turned our world into a winter wonderland. Seanna kept leaping from lap to lap, trying to get a better view of what we were passing. A couple of times, she hopped over the divider to sit with Robert in the driver's seat. He even let her take the reins and guide the sleigh, under close supervision, for a while. We all laughed at the thought of that small little girl controlling those two big horses. I also took this chance to get to know Robert better as we travelled along. His grandfather had passed away about a year before, so his family had sold their small farm to come here and take over his grandpa's farm. It was a much bigger, commercial farm. Robert enjoyed it and hoped to take it over when his father retired. He invited us to all visit some time.

It was two hours later when we finally glided around the corner to the front of the house. We were not ready for the ride to end, but we saw some snowplows headed our way. If we waited too long, then Robert might be stuck by the clear roads and not be able to get the sleigh back to his farm. We probably had about an hour before they cleared the streets he used to get home, so we invited him in for a quick lunch and to warm up a bit before he headed out again.

After lunch, Robert asked if he could give Seanna her gift. She signed the word "yes" and then clapped. He ran out to the sleigh and grabbed a package, which he had wrapped in brown paper and tied with red twine.

"It's not much; I made it myself though," he said proudly.

We all gathered around as Seanna slipped the string off and opened the package. The first thing she pulled out was a handmade stable, followed by all of the other pieces of the nativity. It was obvious he had carved the figures himself, but they were amazing. The faces on the figurines were smooth, round, and not very detailed. He had meticulously painted and carved the bodies and clothes, which were more detailed, to resemble what he pictured those biblical characters to look like. You could tell he had spent a lot of time on them to get them to look just right. The detail on the baby Jesus in Mary's arms was especially beautiful; how he could have carved such a small figure amazed us all. The animals were almost life-like. We passed the figures around so we could all marvel at his talent. I could tell that Seanna was pleased. The hisses and claps were noticeable even through our amazement. Her favorite piece was the angel. She had a hard time letting go of it when Jenny asked if she could see it.

After all of the pieces were neatly placed on the end table, Robert said, with tears in his eyes, "I have one more gift for you to add to your nativity, Seanna. This figure is to help you to always remember, but never to wonder." He pulled out another figure, which he had carefully wrapped in newspaper, from his pocket. The figure resembled three separate people. Robert un-wrapped the figure that looked like a modern-day man, dressed in slacks and a white shirt, and a woman in a white dress holding a baby. Just as the others had been, they had intricate detailing, except for the faces. The man and the woman were hugging and holding the baby between them.

"Remember your family, Seanna, but just like these figures here in this nativity are with Christ, never wonder where your family are. They are with Christ."

Seanna cradled the pieces as if they were her most prized possessions, tears running down her dimpled cheeks. Robert bent down; she buried her face in Robert's shoulder and sobbed. I glanced over at my dad. I had never seen him cry as he was crying now. Robert had touched us all.

After we said our good-byes to Robert and made it back into the house, we all sat down and listened to my mom. She was teaching the stories of the nativity to Seanna, which she had once taught me. Seanna was still cradling the last piece of her gift. After dinner, we let her open some more of her presents from my parents so she could make room for those from Santa. She had asked for nothing but was receiving everything a little girl could want. By bedtime, she could barely stay awake. She fell asleep playing with some of the new dolls she had opened, and I quietly carried her into her room. I was finally able to take the figure of her parents out of her hand after getting her into bed. I placed the handmade carving next to the rest of the nativity set.

There is nothing more magical than a child is on Christmas morning; the excitement, joy, and laughter are unprecedented. It truly was one of the best days of my life. As always, Seanna was the first one out of bed. I heard her in the front room, fiddling with some of the pieces of the nativity she had received from Robert. I am certain she was holding the figure of her parents as she had the night before, so I just let her be alone for a while. After about fifteen minutes, she came running into our room and jumped on me. I caught her just before she landed and tickled her. She sat up and started to sign to me another one of the words she had learned from Robert.

"I don't understand. I forgot that one," I said, puzzled. Seanna gave me a frustrated look.

"It means Santa, Max. It is Christmas, you know," Jenny said sleepily.

"Oh, yeah," I said, trying to hold back a smirk. I pulled the covers back over my head and acted like I wanted to go back to sleep. Seanna would have none of that, though, so she started jumping up and down on top of me as if I were a trampoline.

I laughed and said, "Okay, okay! I give up!" I went to set up the cameras while Jenny kept Seanna busy. With the minutes I then had alone, I glanced at Seanna's nativity and noticed that she had placed a note in between her family and the Christ child. "Love" is what she had written. Looking over the nativity, I compared my current life to my life in the past, right up to a month before. *What a change. I'm happy. Jenny is happy.* Seanna had brought true joy into our lives. Through her love, childhood joy, and notes, she had taught us what mattered most in this life: family, faith, and always keeping kindness in our hearts. The feelings were lasting feelings, not superficial, seasonal ones, almost as if they had become a part of who I was and not just a passing sentiment. I could tell something had changed in me, in my wife, and in all those who had been touched by little notes given by this little angel with no wings.

My parents emerged from the basement "guest room," which I had created by hanging some sheets across the bare studs and framed door. They had heard the commotion in our room and knew the real Christmas fun was about to start. They looked tired but excited.

After Seanna had fallen asleep on Christmas Eve, we, the elves, had given the front room an extreme makeover by hanging more multi-colored lights across the curtain rods and along the pictures hanging on the wall. The lights, along with those on the tree, gave the room the magical glow of red, blue, green, and white; the colors of Christmas were everywhere. There was also some Christmas ribbon, with lights along its length, hanging everywhere else possible, which added to the effect.

Seanna trotted around the room, clapping and pointing at all the extra decorations and signing that Santa had been there. The plate full of chocolate chip cookies that Jenny had helped her set out only had one remaining, and the milk was all gone. The oldest male elf had taken the liberty of tending to that detail with joy the night before. He was thrilled to see Seanna notice his contribution. Next, she pointed to the stockings that were now hanging on the mantle over the fireplace; my mother had sewn five new stockings, with all of our names on them, for this special Christmas. These were not your typical homemade stockings though; she had embroidered images of Christmas over every inch of fabric. I am certain that it took a lot of time to make them. Trust my mom to add her special touch to this occasion. Seanna then moved over to the presents under the tree. She widened her eyes and spread her arms as though to show us that there was an enormous amount of presents. We laughed at her dimpled expression.

"Would you like to open some?" I laughed. Seanna nodded her head "Yes." Then she started digging through the presents under the tree like a dog digging in a gopher hole. She emerged with an armful of presents, but they were not ones addressed to her. She was determined to pass out all of our presents before she opened any of hers.

"Seanna dear, you go ahead and open yours first," Jenny told her, knowing it was of no use. After Seanna had passed out every last present that was not hers, she sat down in front of the tree and motioned to Jenny that we needed to pray.

"That's right, Seanna; we need to give thanks first. Don't we?" my mom said, looking at my dad and me with the partially unwrapped gifts on our laps. I looked at my dad, and he gave me an "oops" look. We set our presents down, and we all knelt down to pray.

After the prayer, paper flew everywhere like it was being spit out of a shredder. My dad and I were like kids; we were just as excited to see what each other had received as what Seanna had received. We kept sneaking peeks and giving nods of approval to our wives, who had obviously done the entire adult-present shopping.

Seanna loved all of the presents that she received, just as I thought she would. I have never seen a more grateful child in my life. After opening each gift, she would inspect every part of it and its newness and then play with it until she lost interest, which usually took thirty to forty minutes. Once she finished with the toy, she would neatly place it on her bed and then go to open a new one. I do not think she had a favorite, but I was glad to see that she played with the baby doll, which came with a bottle and diapers, the longest. That was the only gift that I got her that nobody had prompted me to buy; I thought of that one on my own.

It took almost all day for Seanna to open all her gifts. She never even got dressed. The rest of us just had a relaxing day. My dad and I talked about politics, business, and sports-all the old things we used to talk about-while watching some games on TV. I was glad to have him back in my life. My mom and Jenny visited in the kitchen while fixing the meals most of the day. At times, I would catch Jenny tearing up while looking at Seanna. It was obvious that she loved her and was not looking forward to having to take her back.

Throughout the day, I would watch my family and think, "It doesn't get any better than this."

Finally, after dinner, and after the last of the presents had been opened, we gathered back in the front room where Seanna had returned to play. I had been waiting all day for the time to be right so I could give my surprise note. I figured this was it. I reached into my pocket, and then my dad said, "Now for the last gift of Christmas. I'm not one for notes. I prefer letters." He handed me an envelope. I opened it to find a letter inviting me back to his company as president.

"Dad, I...how...you really want me back...and as the president? Just as an employee would be fine with me." I was shocked.

"I figured you've learned your lesson, and I can't think of any one better; besides, I started to implement some of your suggestions that we talked about on the phone the other day, and you nailed it. Sales are up," he said proudly. I hugged him thankfully. I heard some sniffles as my mom and Jenny started to cry.

"That's nothing to cry about," I laughed. "But I have a gift that is worth crying about," I said, finally seeing my chance to give my surprise. I handed a note to Seanna. She looked at it for a second before deciphering the writing: "Daughter." Seanna broke into tears, and then she slowly came over and hugged Jenny and me. Jenny looked at the note and then at me for an explanation. I nodded my head in a "yes" motion at her smile.

"How did you….when did you…you mean she's ours?" is all Jenny could get out before falling into my arms. Then, Seanna disappeared into her room. Returning she pulled a note from a pocket in her pajamas and gave it to me: "Father." I started to cry now. I was really going to be Seanna's father.

I had finally earned my note. "Thank you, Seanna. Thank you for everything you've done for me and for us. This has been the best Christmas ever." I could barely speak the words through my emotion.

Jenny then mumbled, "It's not over yet." She handed me another note, and I read, "Pregnant." I was stunned. After the years of trying, of being told we could not have children of our own, we would now have two. Miracles truly do happen.

I guess I should not be too surprised though. Christmas is a time for miracles- a time for remembering the beauty, joy, and love that is family. I cannot fully explain the feeling of overwhelming joy and peace that I felt that Christmas season, but I can tell you this much; we have all been given the opportunity to create new beginnings whenever we open our hearts and souls to others. And I sure am thankful that this is just our new beginning instead of

The End.

Dear Reader,

Thank you for taking the time to read *Christmas Notes*. I hope it has enriched your life. I truly felt inspired while writing it. I feel that it is a book that could help people realize what is most important in this life, which I think is especially needed in these times. I am sure you even thought of someone you wanted to share this story with as you were reading. Please help me in spreading the gift of *Christmas Notes*. For more information, go to my website, www.christmasnotes.org.

Acknowledgments

Melissa McKechnie, my editor and friend, thanks for your patience and teachings. American Book Publishing, thank you for giving me a chance to be published. I would also like to thank my beautiful wife, for all her help and support. Thank you to my four children, who inspired me and helped me keep my imagination fresh and pure. I would like to thank my wonderful mother, for her help in making this possible. Next a special note from my heart to my father, who left this life in my youth but his presence is still felt and influence is still strong. And finally to my Savior Jesus Christ who has granted me this small miracle of *Christmas Notes*.

About the Author

Which is mightier: the pipe wrench or the pen? Clint is a talented new author who has been waiting to unleash his craving to write. With a mild case of dyslexia, he was told by a high school counselor the best profession he could pursue would be a truck driver. Clint loves proving that nothing is impossible. He is living proof to never judge a person's creative worth by their profession. Just because someone is doused in plumbing glue does not mean they can't bring the hardest hearts to an emotional connection with a touching story.

Clint dedicates a lot of his time servicing his church. His religious journey started with the death of his father in an industrial accident while Clint was still in high school. His search for the answers to "why" started him on a straight and steady path he has tried to follow ever since.

Clint also has a passion for business, which also lets him explore some of his ingenuity. He has started several businesses during his life, most of which are still successful today. Clint is still very active in his plumbing company. Yes, that is right, he is a plumber, and he loves doing his job...well, most days.